W9-BVT-986

# THE LEFT BEHINDS

## ABE LINCOLN AND THE SELFIE THAT SAVED THE UNION

WITHDRAWN

3 1526 04801403 6

# THE LEFT BEHINDS

**2**

## ABE LINCOLN AND THE SELFIE THAT SAVED THE UNION

### DAVID POTTER

CROWN BOOKS
FOR YOUNG READERS
NEW YORK

Text copyright © 2016 by David Potter
Jacket art copyright © 2016 by C. F. Payne

All rights reserved. Published in the United States by Crown Books for Young Readers, an imprint of Random House Children's Books, a division of Penguin Random House LLC, New York.

Crown and the colophon are registered trademarks of Penguin Random House LLC.

Visit us on the Web! randomhousekids.com

Educators and librarians, for a variety of teaching tools, visit us at RHTeachersLibrarians.com

*Library of Congress Cataloging-in-Publication Data*
Potter, David.
Abe Lincoln and the selfie that saved the Union / David Potter. — First edition.
pages cm. — (The Left Behinds ; 2)
Summary: When the iTime app on their phones sends Mel, Bev, and Brandon to Washington, D.C., in 1863, smack dab in the middle of the Civil War, the youngsters must somehow travel to Gettysburg, make sure what is supposed to happen does happen, save the Union, and be home in time for dinner.
ISBN 978-0-385-39060-6 (trade) — ISBN 978-0-385-39061-3 (lib. bdg.) — ISBN 978-0-385-39062-0 (ebook)
[1. Time travel—Fiction. 2. Adventure and adventurers—Fiction. 3. iPhone (Smartphone)—Fiction. 4. United States—History—Civil War, 1861–1865—Fiction. 5. Gettysburg, Battle of, Gettysburg, Pa., 1863—Fiction. 6. Lincoln, Abraham, 1809–1865—Fiction.] I. Title.
PZ7.P85173Ab 2016  [Fic]—dc23  2015010890

Printed in the United States of America
10 9 8 7 6 5 4 3 2 1
First Edition

For my mother, Ginny Potter

# CONTENTS

**WELCOME TO WASHINGTON CITY**

# ONE

Look—it's not as if I *want* to be a time-traveler or anything. I really have a lot of other things going on that keep me busy, such as school, and, you know, *stuff*. I also happen to be a kid—twelve and three quarters years old, to be exact—which means you can be sure no one is going to *pay* me to go bouncing across the centuries. I don't even get paid for doing chores or homework. And it's not my fault that my phone happens to have an app on it called iTime—it wasn't meant for me, that much I can tell you.

To complicate matters, there are these two other kids—Bev and Brandon—who also have the iTime app on their phones. I wouldn't call them my *friends*, exactly, though we have gotten to know each other a little better since our first adventure. In case you haven't heard about it, we only rescued General George Washington from being shot dead as a doornail and then helped him defeat the Hessians at the Battle of Trenton. So thanks to us, the United States of America is alive and well. And you are very welcome.

We've been thrown together, Bev and Brandon and me. We're the only kids at the Fredericksville School who didn't go home for the Christmas holidays. Our parents are kind of busy, is the thing. So they call us the Left Behinds. Two seconds ago we hit the *Submit* button on our iTime apps and went from the eighteenth century to the twenty-first. The plan was to hop over to the school, grab something to eat, maybe take a hot shower. And then open the presents our parents had shipped, because today still is, after all, Christmas Day.

So we land on our butts, right where we should be—in the basement of Taylor's General Store on the grounds of Washington Crossing Historic Park. The problem is, we're not alone.

There's this crazy old guy who's kind of yelling at us. His name is Professor Moncrieff, and he is the inventor—or the rather the co-inventor, along with his former student—of the iTime app. We've just been told that the former student has Gone Bad. Name of Kurtis. He's out to make a billion dollars or so off the iTime app, for one thing. For another, he intends to go back in time and *change* things. Just to prove that he can cause trouble, because that's what he likes to do.

There's also our teacher, Mr. Hart, whose job is to go with us everywhere. He sort of missed the boat on the time-travel thing, but he did keep in touch via text. And please don't ask me how a guy can text from one century to the next. I don't even know how electricity works, according to Ben Franklin—that's right, *the* Ben Franklin— but I already told that story.

Lastly, there are these military-type guys in the room. Each one wears mirrored sunglasses and stands with his arms folded across his chest. The message: we mean *business*.

"Children," Professor Moncrieff says now. "We do not have all the time in the world. To use the word *time* in its most traditional sense. Please give me your phones. They must be deprogrammed."

*Children?* Who does this old dude think he's talking to—second graders? Give me a break. But the girl child among us—that would be Bev—doesn't seem to take offense. She's smart, Bev is. She's so smart she doesn't ever let you forget it, which is annoying. "What's the hurry?" asks Bev.

Professor Moncrieff doesn't like the question. He frowns, and his dull blue eyes narrow further, if that's even possible. You can tell he thinks Bev's an impertinent smarty-parts.

"We don't have time to debate this!" Professor Moncrieff says. "As we speak, Kurtis is meddling in an event that could prove catastrophic if he is not hunted down and brought to heel. This unauthorized time-travel adventuring must be stopped. My men are professional trackers. They will find Kurtis, I assure you. Now hand over your phones."

"No way," Brandon says. Normally Brandon's a pretty mellow dude. He doesn't worry himself over trifles like homework or good grades. But right now Brandon's not buying it. "How are these guys gonna find him? It's a big country. In any century."

"I have added new functionality—never you mind! Now hand over your phones—or else." He nods his head at his three goons—I mean his three professional *trackers*—who each take a menacing step toward us.

"You can have this," I say, and open up the leather satchel I happen to be carrying with me. I snatched the satchel from a Mr. Kramm, who was Kurtis's right-hand man back in 1776. Stenciled on the outside are the letters T.G.W., INC., which stand for Things Go Wrong, Incorporated. That's Kurtis's idea of a joke.

Inside are papers, maps, gold coins, and extra bullets. I take out a handful of the gold coins, put them in my pocket—hey, you never know—and toss the satchel on the ground. "I don't want it," I say. "And I don't want this either." I also happen to have taken Mr. Kramm's German Luger, a World War II–era pistol. I figure nothing good is going to come from my hanging on to it.

Neither Professor Moncrieff nor his men seem impressed. They just want our phones. Mr. Hart doesn't seem to know what to do. At this point he is—to use one of Bev's favorite expressions—totally *useless*.

But who's got more of a stake in history going right than us?

So Bev speaks up. Her mom is an actress. In Hollywood. You probably heard of her, though she hasn't appeared in much recently. Bev *says* she hates movies, Hollywood, celebrity, and the whole stupid thing, but you know what? She's got the acting thing going on herself. Like right now, she strikes her Miss Defiant pose.

"You mean *these* phones?" Bev says, and holds up her phone. But she doesn't hold it up in an act of submission. She holds it up so she can *look* at it.

And we know *exactly* what she's looking at.

The iTime app. The one that caused all the trouble in the first place.

Brandon and I hold up our own phones, and we see the familiar five boxes. All filled in. DAY is *1*. MONTH is *7*. And YEAR is *1863*.

1863?

Who set the iTime app for 1863?

The fourth box, TIME, is set at *11:00 a.m.* And the last box, COORDINATES, says *38.8591° N, 77.0367° W.*

The *Submit* button is at the bottom.

It's crystal clear. We can hand our phones over to the professor, or press *Submit*.

And zoom off to 1863. Destination unknown.

It looks like we're going to have about three seconds to decide this thing.

Make it two seconds.

Professor Moncrieff shouts, "NO, NOT AGAIN!"

Call it one second.

Mr. Hart shouts, "DON'T!"

But we're modern kids. We ourselves have been sort of programmed. We even have T-shirts for moments like these.

Just do it.

So we do.

# TWO

TIME TRAVEL, I'M HERE to tell you, is not for wimps. It's like we're thrown into a roller coaster speeding along at warp speed in total darkness.

We don't know up from down, our stomachs go haywire, we worry about losing our lunch.

Then *boom*, we land. Bumpity bumpity bump, times three behinds.

Three sore behinds for the Left Behinds.

Now I'm starting to notice things about this time-travel business. The first time was a complete blur—we were ninety-five percent dazed, and our short-term memory was completely *fried*.

But this trip? I'm ready for action from the get-go. I already know *when* we are—July 1, 1863—but as of yet I have no clue *where* we are.

I stand up. So do Bev and Brandon.

First thing we notice: it is hot. H, O, T, hot. Blast-furnace hot. But only a few minutes ago—or a couple of hundred years, depending on how you want to look at it—we were cold, cold, cold. Frozen-toes-and-fingertips-and-nose cold. We were still dressed for that occasion, not this one. In our winter gear, basically.

Second thing we notice: we're in the middle of a road, it seems like, surrounded on all sides by a bunch of people going about their business. The men are wearing full suits and hats, the women long dresses and bonnets. Even though it's steaming, no one's in shorts or flip-flops.

And bearing down upon us, at what seems like a hundred miles an hour, a horse and buggy.

Two horses, one buggy.

"Watch it!" I yell, and grab for Bev.

She's two steps ahead of me, of course. She's already stepped aside and dragged Brandon with her.

Which means there's nothing between me and two horses coming down full bore.

Somebody yanks on the reins, the buggy lurches, the left side lifts off the road, and then the whole thing tips over. Out of the corner of my right eye, I see a flash of someone *jumping* from the carriage.

Four horse feet, clod with muddy horseshoes, punch the air inches from my face. Then all four land on the ground, and each horse gives a short snort.

I don't get a second, even, to be grateful that I haven't been clomped in two, because there's this guy shouting in my face, and, to the side, a woman screaming her head off.

She was the one who had jumped out of the buggy, and she must have landed hard. Blood's gushing down her forehead. She's sitting on the dirt road, her brown flouncy dress all akimbo, and the bonnet she had been wearing now dangling off her neck.

"You little . . . you little . . . I'll have your hide!" shouts the driver of the buggy. Brandon tells the guy to back off.

And the bonnet lady is wailing now louder than *ever*.

I'm thinking, *Hey, we just got here, you know? So would everyone kind of just chillax for a sec?*

"Mel, you okay?'" says Bev, tugging at my sleeve.

Then two crowds gather: one around the lady who jumped out of the carriage, and one around me.

The crowd around the lady is kind, caring, concerned.

The one around me? Not so much.

Though the buggy driver is still yelling in my face, I am able, despite the racket, to notice a few things.

He's yelling at me in English, so we can all speak the local lingo. Good thing we didn't transport to someplace where we wouldn't know what's going on, like Moscow or Bangkok or Cairo.

But everyone seems way more upset than absolutely necessary. I mean, come on, the lady has a cut on her forehead, and she's bleeding, but it's not as if she's *dead.*

"You nearly killed her!" the driver is still screaming. He's five two, maybe, this guy. Patchy gray beard. He's wearing a dusty black hat that's seen better times. Then he yells, "It's the First Lady! You nearly killed Mrs. Lincoln! You will pay for this, you . . . you unwashed heathen!"

# THREE

FIRST LADY?

Mrs. *Lincoln*?

Oh boy.

"Take it easy," Brandon says to the driver, trying to loom large. Brandon's kind of big, but he's still only twelve, so no one pays him any mind.

The lady—this would be Mrs. Lincoln—wails again, and everyone turns their attention her way. "Mrs. Lincoln," someone says. "Mrs. Lincoln, are you all right?"

"Does it look like it?" Mrs. Lincoln snarls. It's definitely not her indoor voice. "I had to jump out of my carriage ... because ... because ... we were going to CRASH! McGee! What in the world were you thinking? I could have been killed!"

All eyes swing to Mr. McGee, the driver of the rig. The coachman, I believe is what they call themselves. "Ma'am," he says. "It wasn't my fault, beg pardon. I was riding along, sweet as could be, when out of nowhere these children appeared right in front of me! A miracle it was I could hold back the horses from running 'em over! They could've been killed!"

"What about me?" Mrs. Lincoln pouts. "*I* could have been killed! And I may be yet, if this wound in my head isn't attended to."

"Is there a doctor?" someone shouts. "We have an emergency! The First Lady requires immediate attention!"

Everyone starts shouting again until a guy comes forward. "I am Dr. Nelson," the guy says. "I am a surgeon with the Sixty-Seventh Regiment New York Volunteers. Let me through, I say. Let me through!"

Dr. Nelson rushes to the side of Mrs. Lincoln. He carefully turns her head this way and that. Then he takes out a very white handkerchief from his coat pocket and begins cleaning the wound on her forehead.

"Mel, I think we're in Washington," Bev says. "In 1863. That's in the middle of the Civil War, right?"

"Right," I say. "Anyone have an idea what we're doing here?"

"I do," Brandon says.

"You have an idea, Brandon?" says Bev. "There's a newsflash for you."

"Funny, Bev. As in not very. But just remember this:

if we're here for a reason, it can't be a good one. Just like last time."

I have a thought—that maybe we should slink away now while we have the chance—but then, we stand accused. The First Lady's coachman, McGee, points at us and says, "Those are the ones that caused it all. They shouldn't be allowed to roam the streets, thievin' at will!"

We're grabbed, by the shoulders, at exactly the same time Dr. Nelson helps Mrs. Lincoln to her feet. "I am taking her to the Carver Army Hospital," Dr. Nelson says. "'Tis around the corner. I must bandage her wound and then I shall personally bring her back to the White House."

He very gingerly puts his arm around Mrs. Lincoln's shoulder and starts to lead her away. "It's not far, ma'am. It won't take us a minute."

"They ought to be thrown in jail," says Coachman McGee. "They're ratty little varmints, they are. They'd steal the lint out of your pockets, I swear they would!"

"Wait!" Mrs. Lincoln cries. Dr. Nelson takes his arm away from her shoulders, but the hands around our collars don't loosen a millimeter. "Why are these . . . *children* being manhandled so?"

"They're about to be arrested, ma'am," Coachman McGee says. "On account of them being the ones who caused your accident. It must have been part of a plan they had, begging your pardon, ma'am, some thievin' scheme no doubt, to lift your purse or your belongings."

"Oh, what nonsense, McGee," Mrs. Lincoln says, and

takes a few steps toward us. "Now then, let me look at these children."

She stands before us, Mary Todd Lincoln, the First Lady of the United States, the wife of Abraham. She's very short, and not exactly thin, but she does not look upon us unkindly. She examines me first, then Bev, and then spends a very, very long time gazing upon Brandon.

We're not really dressed for the time and place, remember. We just crossed the Delaware River in an icy storm, marched nine miles to Trenton, and won the battle that saved the Revolution. So not a single item of our clothing is right for this time or this place. No wonder everyone's looking at us like we're from Mars or someplace.

Mrs. Lincoln is still checking out Brandon. Dr. Nelson is on one side, Coachman McGee is on the other, and now everybody is examining Brandon like he's a medical curiosity. He is kind of a head case, if you want to know the truth. No one knows for sure what's going on inside his noggin, probably not even Brandon himself.

He holds his hands up. "I don't bite," he says. "Honest."

"Dear boy," Mrs. Lincoln says. "You look so very familiar. Have we met?"

"I don't believe we have, ma'am," Brandon says. "In fact, I'm pretty sure we haven't."

"Do you have folk here?" she asks.

"Well, not really. My dad passed. And my mom's in New Mexico."

"New Mexico? The territory? Gracious me. Isn't it *hostile*? However could anyone *be* from there?"

"Well," Brandon begins, "it's kind of a long story." By now Bev and I are trying to send Brandon signals—grunts, eyebrow raises, coughs, etc. We're trying to tell him not to forget that there's a slight discrepancy—a hundred and fifty years or so—between how he sees things and how she sees things.

"And why are you in Washington City?" she says. "Dressed in these ... odd clothes? Does your mother know you're here?"

"Well, not exactly."

"Have you run away, lad? Have you come to join the Union Army, against your mother's wishes?"

Now Brandon glances over to us, and I give him a quick headshake *no*. If there's one thing I'm sure of, it's that we don't want to join any man's army, not after what we've been through. None of us are even near *legal* yet.

"No, ma'am," Brandon says. "We didn't come to join the army."

Mrs. Lincoln moves ever closer to Brandon and looks deeply into his eyes. "I swear I have seen you before," she says. "Did you know Willie? Were you friends with my dear boy?"

The crowd surrounding us falls silent, and not in a good way. More like in a very *eerie* way. Like everyone takes in a deep breath and no one wants to be the first to let it out.

Before Brandon can provide an answer, Mrs. Lincoln says, "Hush." She places her right hand on Brandon's face. Then she does something weird.

As in extremely weird, and more than a little creepy.

It's like she goes into a *trance* or something.

She *mumbles* some words.

Sways back and forth.

Then her eyes open wide, and she says, "He's spoken. My poor dead son Willie has spoken to me through this boy!"

# FOUR

Mrs. Lincoln collapses to the ground, her right forearm theatrically pressed against her forehead, her left arm waving in the air, as if warding away something bad. "It's no good!" she cries. "They'll never let him out! My dear, dear boy!"

"The spirits have taken possession!" someone yells from the crowd.

"Back!" commands Dr. Nelson. "Back away, I say! Mrs. Lincoln needs air! Or she shall succumb!"

Everyone clears some space, Bev, Brandon, and me included. Especially the three of us. 'Cause the one thing we particularly don't *need* at this particular *moment* is, you know, a *scene*. Especially not with the First Lady of the United States. Who seems to be a little *touched* in the *head*.

We start slinking away, hoping that no one notices. If we can get five or six steps from the crowd, then we can turn and make a run for it.

"Mrs. Lincoln," says Dr. Nelson, "we must get you to Carver Hospital. I fear you have a contusion on the top of your head. It must be cleaned and dressed. I urge you, ma'am. In the strongest possible terms. Please come with me at once to the hospital."

We're at the back edge of the crowd when Mrs. Lincoln shouts, "Where have those children gone? I will not let them out of my sight!"

The crowd parts like the Red Sea, and there we are, in no-man's-land.

And of course just at *this* moment—when all eyes are on us, and all is silent—we hear a familiar melody.

A little tri-tone melody. Almost like this: *ba-da-bing!*

Naturally it has to be *my* phone that goes off, not Bev's or Brandon's. Mrs. Lincoln, still sitting in the road, raises her finger and points to me. "What," she says, "in heaven's name was that *sound*?"

"Sound?" I say. "What sound?"

"It's a sign!" she cries. "That sound! A signal, from the beyond! Willie calls to me!"

"Mrs. Lincoln," Dr. Nelson says, "it is most urgent that we get you to Carver Hospital. Most urgent!" He starts to help her up, but she shakes her head and tries to push him away.

"Come here, child," Mrs. Lincoln says to me. "I want to look at you."

I come forward, and Mrs. Lincoln pats the ground beside her, so I sit. Then she puts her hand on my face, as she put it on Brandon's. She holds it there for a very uncomfortable few seconds, and frowns.

"You did not hear a sound?" she asks. "Like a bell, but not a bell?"

I know you're not supposed to lie. George Washington—who you could say I happen to know personally—supposedly never lied, and Mrs. Lincoln's husband, of course, is known as Honest Abe. On the other hand, I didn't think now was exactly the right time to spring the truth on Mrs. Abraham Lincoln, so I maybe kind of stretched it a little. I said, "I didn't hear any sound, ma'am. Not a single thing."

"You didn't hear a tiny bell sound?"

"No."

"Are you certain?"

"Yes."

Her hand is still on my face, remember. At first it was a gentle touch. Now, each time I say no, she presses her fingers deeper into my skin.

"He's hiding something," she finally says, and takes her hand away. "He knows more than he says! Have you seen Willie? Have you spoken to him! Tell me! I demand it!"

The crowd moves in. I thought it was hot before, but it feels as if the temperature just shot up thirty degrees or so. I can tell because I'm sweating. My hands, my face, my back, my feet.

"These are awfully strange clothes you're wearing,"

Mrs. Lincoln says. She moves her hand from my face to my jacket. "Awfully strange. These children are dressed as if for winter. Has not anyone noticed?"

She's getting herself a little worked up now, and Dr. Nelson does two things at once: one, he helps Mrs. Lincoln to her feet, and two, he shoves me away.

I'm okay with that. I don't take it personally. I brush myself off and give a nod to Bev and Brandon.

This time we're really going to have to make a break for it. But before we can make a move, our plans change. Or should I say, get changed.

Mrs. Lincoln points to the three of us and says, "Those children! Bring them back! All of them! I want them to come to the White House!"

# FIVE

**W**HAT THE FIRST LADY wants, we find out pretty quick, the First Lady gets.

We have to wait about a half hour at Carver Hospital while Dr. Nelson dresses Mrs. Lincoln's wounds, then they find a cart, not a carriage, to haul Mrs. Lincoln and Dr. Nelson and the three of us from the hospital to the White House. We sit in the back, next to bags of potatoes and baskets of apples. I'm not one to complain, but those apples? They're a smidge on the *ripe* side, I think. I don't know if they're meant for people or for horses.

So now we're going down Fourteenth Street—I know this because that's where Dr. Nelson told the driver to go—but nothing looks like the Washington D.C. I saw two years ago, when I went to the Air and Space Museum with my parents, which was the first time we did something fun together since I don't know when. Anyway, Fourteenth Street is basically a dusty unpaved road. The buildings are plain wooden structures, for the most part, that look like they'd fall over at the first sign of wind. Clumps of people clog up the sidewalk. A *lot* of people. And every single one of them looks like they just stepped out of a book of Civil War photos. It kind of seems as if the whole city is in black and white, not color, but maybe that's because everyone, with the exception of Mrs. Lincoln, is dressed totally in *black*. And they aren't even trying to be cool, either.

"What's up with Mrs. Lincoln?" Bev says. "Was she trying to talk to *dead people*?"

"I don't know," Brandon says. "I just know that when she had her hand on my face I was really starting to get the creeps."

"I was worried," I say, "that she was going to read your mind. And that would really have put her over the top."

"Fortunately," Bev says, "there's not a lot to read there. Like, nothing."

"Funny, Bev," said Brandon. "And then you got a text, Mel. That helped. I thought they were going to frisk us on the spot."

"Oh yeah, the text," I said, pulling out my phone. "Almost forgot." We all look at it.

It's from Mr. Hart, naturally.

*Why did you leave? I had everything under control. Reprogram your phones and return here immediately.*

"I don't think so," Bev says. "We'll just find ourselves with that crazy Professor Moncrieff and those military guys. I'm not sure Mr. Hart is a hundred percent in charge of things either."

"Mr. Hart's worried about getting in trouble with the school," I say. "Everything else is out of his range."

"But why do you think we're here?" Bev says. "Why July 1, 1863? What's so significant about this day?"

"Maybe we should ask Mr. Hart," Brandon says. It seems as good an idea as any, so I send this:

*Mr. Hart—why are we here? What's supposed to happen this time?*

He sends his reply right away:

*Never you mind. Reprogram your phones and come back this instant!*

"Maybe that means he doesn't know himself," I say. "But I'm pretty sure 1863 isn't an accident, or just a random date. It's got to be specific to something."

"What is?" says Brandon.

"This date. That guy they were talking about—Kurtis—he wouldn't pick any old date. He must have picked this one. But why?"

No one had an answer. I text Mr. Hart: *We're going to look around.* Then I turn off my phone, and tell Bev and Brandon to do the same, so we don't run our batteries down.

Our cart turns to the right, and finally we're on a paved road. The buildings now are a little spiffier—some are made of brick, and don't look like they'll fall over—and I realize we've just turned onto Pennsylvania Avenue. One building sells guns. It's got a large sign: PISTOLS, PISTOLS, PISTOLS! COLTS, NAVY, AND POCKET REVOLVERS, LATEST IMPROVEMENTS. ALSO SHARPS REPEATING PISTOLS, WITH THE NECESSARY APPENDAGES. FOR SALE LOW. I wouldn't call it the snappiest sign I've ever seen, but if I were looking to buy a pistol, that would be the place I'd go.

Up front we hear Mrs. Lincoln say something, and then Dr. Nelson turns around. "The First Lady wants you to get yourselves ready," he says. "To be as presentable as you can."

"It's really, really hot," Brandon says. "I need some relief." He removes his jacket and his hoodie, and I do the same. We toss them aside. Bev also takes off her jacket, but she folds it very carefully and puts it on the cart beside her. Underneath all that, we're wearing regular shirts and pants. Regular, that is, for our time, not theirs. Brandon keeps his red hat on, of course. If I could find a pair of shorts, I'd wear them, even if I were the only person in the whole city wearing them. It's that kind of hot.

"Remember, there are rules," Dr. Nelson says, relaying instructions from Mrs. Lincoln. "No loud voices, no running, no touching anything that doesn't belong to you, no using your hands to wipe your mouths, and if you must ask a question, you will raise your hand and wait until you are recognized. Is all this clear?"

"Where we going again?" Brandon asks Dr. Nelson. "To jail?"

Before he can respond, the answer is before us. It's set back, and has a lawn in front of it. The building that looks pretty much the same as ever. The good old White House.

The cart pulls into a circular driveway and up to the White House entrance. As we get closer we see a few people peering at us, not quite sure, I suppose, who we are or why a vegetable cart is transporting Mrs. Lincoln. Then a little kid comes bursting through a side door and tearing across the lawn. He's maybe nine, ten years old, and dressed up as a miniature Union soldier: blue coat with white shoulder straps, a blue cap, a wide black belt with a huge silver buckle, and white gloves pulled up to his elbows. He's yelling at the top of his lungs, which we were just told was against all the rules. "Mother! Mother!" the boy shouts, pointing at Bev and Brandon and me. "Who have you brought to play?"

# SIX

**T**HEN THE KID TAKES a running leap right into the back of the cart. He lands half in Bev's lap and half in a sack of potatoes. Now, if anyone knows *anything* about Bev, which this kid obviously does not, this just isn't the best way to introduce yourself.

"Excuse me!" Bev says, pushing the kid off her.

"Mother!" he yells. "Did you bring me friends? Did you, Mother, did you? Come on, let's play—I know just the thing! Let's go to the fort!" And then the boy starts yanking first Brandon and then me by the arm. "Come on, hurry! No time to waste! Those Rebs might attack at any time! We got to defend Washington City!"

"Now, Tad," Mrs. Lincoln says, turning in her seat. "Let's just you calm down now. I'm going to want to talk to these children myself before too long—"

"Mother!" interrupts the boy—Tad, as Mrs. Lincoln calls him. "What happened to your head? You've been hit by enemy fire!" Then he climbs over the apples and potatoes and flings himself into Mrs. Lincoln's arms, nearly knocking her over. Dr. Nelson tries to peel him off, but now we are surrounded by five or six people who I assume work at the White House—cooks and groundskeepers, by the way they're dressed. Everyone wants to know why Mrs. Lincoln has a bandage on her head, why is she being driven around in a vegetable cart, and what happened to Mr. McGee and the carriage. Who we are, and what we're doing here, seems to be the last thing on anyone's mind.

"A carriage accident," Dr. Nelson says. "A slight wound to the forehead, nothing overly serious, though I recommend that she lie down a spell. Now, Tad, if you don't mind," he adds, "I do believe your mother could use some peace and quiet."

"She's going to be all right?" Tad asks, and when Dr. Nelson nods his head Tad unlocks his grip around his mother and bounds into the back of the cart again.

"Come on, let's go up to the fort! Before it's too late! Can I bring them, Mother? Can I, please? Oh, please say I can. I can't wait to show them the fort!"

"Well," Mrs. Lincoln says, adjusting her bonnet, which was thrown askew by Tad's embrace. "I don't suppose it would hurt any. And I might have a chance to recover myself, like you say, Doctor. I do believe I feel a pounder coming on. Right here, on the top of my head."

"I need assistance!" Dr. Nelson says. "Mrs. Lincoln

must rest." The assembled cooks and gardeners rush forward to help Mrs. Lincoln from the cart.

Tad, meanwhile, has taken her answer as a yes, and is very determinedly pulling Brandon and me off the cart. He's a small kid, but very, very energetic. I'm not sure if he's always this way or if he's just excited to show us his fort.

"Take it easy, little bud," says Brandon. "I'm coming already." Brandon hops off the cart, I hop off, and Bev descends, like a queen who's had enough of the peasants. But Tad grabs her hand anyway and starts tugging her along to the White House.

Yeah, *that* White House. I think all three of us are having trouble processing this. We can't just walk in there like we own the place, can we?

We can. Tad can, I mean. And since we're with him, no one seems to mind as we go charging through the door.

Not walking, politely and respectfully, per Mrs. Lincoln's instructions.

*Charging.*

We don't even have the time to grab our jackets and hoodies, not that we need them. But it's becoming clear that this kid operates by a different set of rules than everyone else. I suppose when you're the son of the president of the United States, no one's going to tell you what *not* to do, but Brandon, Bev, and I have become so accustomed to following all the many, many rules at the Fredericksville School, we're having trouble adjusting. Not that Tad cares or even takes notice.

"Come on come on come on!" Tad yells happily. "Hurry! No time to lose!" We race down one hall, turn a corner, go up one staircase, we go up a second staircase, then we climb a narrow staircase into what seems to be an attic, and then one final metal staircase and voilà—we're on the roof of the White House. No one said a word as we trampled our way up, or told us to walk, not run.

Whoa.

The sky is blue blue blue, and laid out before us is what they call Washington City. We want to pause a moment to get our bearings, but Tad, naturally, is already running full tilt to the far corner of the roof. "Come on come on come on!" he shouts. "You have to see!"

Along the edge of the top of the White House—in case you've never been there, which I kind of doubt you have—there are spindly wooden things, kind of like bowling pins, called *balusters*. And all these balusters put together form what's called a *balustrade*.

This is according to Bev, anyway, who says she knows this kind of stuff. The balustrade on top of the White House is maybe three feet high, so you can see over, and you can also see *through* it, as one baluster is maybe eight or ten inches from the next one.

Tad has turned it into a pretty nifty *fort*.

"Look," Tad says. "Muskets and cannon! And I got a pistol too! We'll let 'em have it with everything we got, soon as the Rebs show their eyes!" He picks up one of the muskets, pokes it through a space between two balusters, and says, "That's Virginia right over there! Come on, you Rebs! I dare you!"

The "Rebs" he's referring to, of course, are the soldiers of the Confederate Army—we are in the middle of the Civil War, after all.

I don't think Tad's musket is loaded, or can even fire—it's beat up and rusted out. And the "cannon" he has is a painted two-by-four plank of wood. But he's determined. There's no doubting that.

He stops a second, in the midst of his battle plans, and looks us up and down. "Where you from? Have you seen any fighting? And why you dressed so odd? Are you in disguise?"

"Well," I tell him, "I wouldn't say we're in disguise, exactly."

"Are you scouts? Spies? Are you traveling behind the lines, finding out what Johnny Reb's up to?"

"Nope, nothing like that. We're just . . . what are we? Bev? Brandon?"

"We're tourists," Brandon tells him. "Kind of."

"Tourists?"

"Yeah. We just wander around from place to place."

Tad's eyes go wide; his mouth drops open. "You mean it?" he says.

"I mean it," says Brandon. "Every day's a new day. We never know where we're going to be. And I'm not kidding." Brandon eyes Bev and me, and raises his eyebrows. Then he winks.

"Can I go with you?" Tad says. "I'm just itching for an adventure! I'd go anywhere, I'd join up right today, if I could just get ahold of some Rebs. They're not only out there, you know," he says, "across the Potomac and all, but they're also right here, in Washington City. I heard Pa say so, I heard him say so a thousand times—Washington City is full of liars and spies! Like the society lady they found had given the enemy our war plans before the Battle of Bull Run! And that's why we got ambushed and had to turn tail and run. I saw our men when they came back across the Long Bridge, all shot to pieces!"

Tad points, and across the landscape of Washington City we see the Potomac River, winding around like a snake, and in the distance we can make out what looks to be a very modest bridge, which, at the moment, seemed to be heavily traveled.

"Man," Brandon says. "Look at that—it's nowhere near done!" He points, and we notice the Washington Monument, which is maybe a quarter built. Maybe less than a quarter. And surrounding the stubby marble monument-in-waiting are what look to be vast wooden structures. From which I hear—unless I'm mistaken—very loud, and very distinct, mooing.

As in cows.

I look more closely: a thousand, maybe two thousand cows, packed together. I think they're eating the grass.

"Course they're not done with the monument," says Tad. "They stopped working on it years ago. Pa says they plumb ran out of money, and now with the war, nobody's brave enough to finish it because they might get shot by all the Confederates nearby."

"What's with all those cows?" Bev says.

"It's the stockyard, of course," Tad says. "Pa told me they slaughter near two hundred cows every day over there. And he says that ain't near enough, sometimes. Soldiers got to get their rations of beef along with everything else. Ma says when an army of men come to town it's worse than a hundred plagues of locusts. The soldier boys get themselves into everything, and I mean everything."

Brandon thinks cows grazing across from the White House is so very, very interesting that he needs to take a picture. So he takes out his phone, turns it on, lines up his shot, and snaps one off. Completely forgetting, of course, that we're in 1863. Instagram hasn't even been invented yet.

Tad notices, of course. Tad steps back and says to Brandon, "What's that thing in your hands?"

"Oh," Brandon says sheepishly. He's just been busted. Bev rolls her eyes, and so do I.

"It's nothing."

"Well, it's something, not nothing," says Tad. "Let me see it."

Brandon lets down his hand and his guard at the same

time. I think we've all underestimated the determination of a nine-year-old kid who has free rein of the White House. Tad doesn't ask again; instead he snatches Brandon's phone from his hands and runs to the far corner of the roof.

"Great move, Brandon," Bev says. "You know he's never seen an iPhone before, right?"

"I forgot," Brandon says.

"Um," I say. "I don't think this is a really good idea. What if he decides to show it to his dad?"

Tad's dad, of course, only happens to be Abraham Lincoln, the sixteenth president of these United States. I don't believe he's ever seen an iPhone either.

"We're going to have to get it back," Bev says. "One way or another."

# SEVEN

WE FIND TAD AT the very farthest corner of the roof. As we approach we can see that he's trying to figure out what Brandon's phone *does*. He's even taken off his white officer's gloves, the ones that come nearly to his elbow, so he can free up his fingers to poke around.

"Tad," says Brandon. "Give it back, please. You shouldn't grab things, you know. It's not polite."

Tad gives no indication that he's heard Brandon, or, if he has, cares. He's turning the phone backwards and forwards, this way and that way.

"What is this thing?" he says. "You sure it doesn't belong to the government?"

"It belongs to me," Brandon says. He steps a little closer, so he's practically towering over Tad. "Now give it back."

"I won't, not till I show Pa. I bet he knows what it's for. I'm beginning to think you all are up to something. What did you say your names were again?"

"I'm Brandon," says Brandon. "He's Mel and she's Bev. Now give me back my phone or . . ."

"Your what?" Tad says. "Your *phone*? Is that what this is called?"

"Nice job, Brandon," says Bev, who gets a glare in response.

"You need to give that back, Tad," I say. "It doesn't belong to you. You can't go around just snatching things out of people's hands."

"Pa says I can do whatever I want," Tad says. His little jaw is set in pure defiance. "So there."

"I doubt it," Bev says. "No parent would say that. If we tell him you stole something, I'm sure you'll get yourself in a lot of trouble."

"Will not!" says Tad. "Pa never yells at me. Never never never!"

"Then we'll tell your mother," I say. "I'm sure she won't be happy."

"You better not!" Tad says, alarmed. "You have no right—I don't even know who you are or what you're doing here!"

"You invited us, Tad, remember?" I say. "You grabbed our arms and told us to come on up here. Now, if you just give it back to Brandon, everything will be cool."

"Cool? How's it going to be cool? Can't you tell it's hot?"

"He means *fine*," Bev says. "Everything will be fine if you just give it back. We won't have to tell your mother or anyone else."

"Why's it got all these pictures on it?" Tad asks.

"Give it back and we'll tell you," Brandon says.

"Tell me first and then maybe I will," Tad counters.

"All right," says Brandon, "I'll tell you what it is—it's a picture taker. Now give it back."

"Can't be a picture taker—it's too small. You're lyin'. I can tell. Pa always tells me to watch out for people who lie. Watch your wallet, he says. That's usually what they're after. I'm beginning to think that maybe you three aren't even who you say you are. Maybe you're Reb spies. If I tell Pa, you'll be hanged, all three of you!"

"Of course we're not spies," Bev says. "Do we *look* like spies? We're just children, like you. We go to school. In New Jersey."

"School? What school?"

"The Fredericksville School," Bev says.

"I've never heard of it," Tad says, which isn't surprising, since it won't be founded until 1876. But I know what Bev's trying to do—keep him talking until we can make a grab for Brandon's phone. "And how do I know you're telling me the truth, anyway? If you're spies, you're liable to say anything. It's why Pa has made near everyone in Washington City sign the oath. You can't trust anyone these days. And you've already lied to me once, by trying to say this here thing is a *picture taker*. So I say you're spies, and spies you are, until proven otherwise. Or until you sign the oath."

"Oath?" I say. "What oath?

"Why, the Ironclad Oath," Tad says. "You mean to say you never heard of it? That just about proves it right there. You're spies, all three of you. And you brought trouble right up to the White House, didn't you?"

"You invited us up," Brandon says. "We were just minding our own business."

"Oh sure," says Tad. "Just minding your own business—no one is going to believe that. Not especially when you brought up this black thing and tried to pass it off as a *picture taker*. Now, just what is this thing? Are you going to tell me the truth? Or are you going to lie?"

The three of us have got him surrounded now. Tad is impulsive, for sure, but he's not dumb—he figures out what we're up to and makes a break for it before we can retake Brandon's phone. He zigs right, past Bev, who makes a lame lunge for him and misses. One down.

The kid's got an advantage, we quickly realize—he knows the roof of the White House and we don't. But there's three of us and only one of him, and because we're older we ought to be faster, stronger, and smarter. Right?

Wrong. Local knowledge, it turns out, trumps faster-stronger-smarter every time. Brandon is slow off the mark and tries to follow. There's all kinds of stuff besides bal-usters on the roof—smokestacks, for example. Tad goes to the right, then dodges a short stubby smokestack on his left. Brandon goes right after the first one, but that's about all the dodge he has in him. Instead of going left around the next one, he goes straight into the smokestack and falls over.

Two down.

That leaves me.

The kid is maybe twenty yards from the doorway to the staircase.

Maybe fifteen yards ahead of me.

I do the math: he'll get to the door before I get to him. After that, there's no telling where he'll go. There's the short staircase leading from the roof to the attic, but after that, I'll be lost.

Tad won't. I'm sure he knows every room and every corner of the White House. I don't even remember the way we came up.

So it's one of those now-or-never type of things.

If the kid gets loose in the White House, we might never get Brandon's phone back.

And now he's ten yards from the door. Which means right about now I've got to think of something.

"Stop!" I yell. "You have to stop! It's a bomb! Or else the whole place is going to blow to smithereens!"

Tad stops.

He's five feet, at most, from the door. I'm fifteen feet away. There's no doubt if he wanted to, he could go through the door and down the stairs and away he'd be.

"Let me have it," I say. "It's set to go off any minute.

You bring it down there and there's no telling what might happen. Could be the end of the war right there. You don't want that, do you?"

Tad turns to face me. His hands are trembling, and his face has turned white. "You are spies, then," he says. "And I brought you right in."

"Tad," I say, "you got it right and you got it wrong. We *are* spies. But just not for the Rebs. Now give me that thing."

"You mean . . . you mean you all are *Union* spies?"

"That's right. And you've blown our cover. Also, you activated a bomb that was only supposed to be used as a last resort. Not here, not at the White House."

"Where then?" he asks.

I jerk my thumb backward. "Out there. But only if worse came to worst. And only if we could get it . . . um . . . close enough to make a difference."

"You mean you're fixing to blow up General Lee?"

"I can't say any more. I've already told you too much. Orders. Now hand it over so we can deactivate it. And you better hurry. By my calculations we have about twenty seconds till she blows."

Tad thrusts Brandon's iPhone at me, and I take it.

Brandon and Bev come up alongside us. "Here you go, Brandon," I say, handing him his phone. "Put in the code and deactivate the bomb."

Tad is wide-eyed now. Astonished. Brandon takes his phone and furiously taps away.

"Is the bomb deactivated, Brandon?" I ask.

"Yep," Brandon says. "All clear."

"And we had just seconds to spare," I say. "That was cutting it close. Tad, you have to be more careful. And now we're going to have to make you take a vow of secrecy. You mentioned that everyone had to sign the what, the Ironclad Oath?"

"That's right, every single person in the government had to sign it, and even some folks not in government, on account of they was acting suspicious."

"Hold up your right hand, Tad," I say. He brings himself to rigid attention and holds his right hand high.

"Repeat after me: 'I, Tad Lincoln, do solemnly swear . . .'"

"I, Tad Lincoln," Tad says, "do solemnly swear . . ."

"'That I will not divulge any secrets nor any information *whatsoever* learned here this day, July first, 1863 . . .'"

He repeats, mangling only a few words along the way. I give him the rest: "'So help me God.'"

"So help me God," Tad says. Then, to seal the deal, I spit into my palm, Tad does the same, and we shake.

Bev frowns. She doesn't even have to say what she's thinking, because it's written all over her face. But right now nothing is more important than having Tad on our side, and having Tad keeping his little trap shut, especially about Brandon's iPhone. If a little spit helps the cause, then Bev is going to have to live with it.

"I think we need to get off the roof," Bev says. "And go about our business."

That's a very good point, although we're not sure exactly what our business here is. But Tad has a suggestion.

"Let's go say howdy to Pa!" he says. "He don't mind if I interrupt even though he's got a country to run—tells me so all the time! Come on, let's go! Last one down the stairs is a rotten egg!"

# EIGHT

And then Tad breaks for the rooftop door. We have no choice except to follow.

Down the metal staircase we go, first into the White House attic, but just like on the way up, Tad has no intention of stopping here. He heads straight down to the next floor, marches through a door, and then holds his position.

He's peering around a corner. He turns around, to make sure we're right behind him, and then puts a finger to his lips. "Shhhh!" Tad says, very loudly. "Pa's office is straight across the hall. We need to make a run for it, 'cause there's enemies all over! On the count of three, all right? One, two, three, go!"

Then Tad bursts into the hallway, cuts to his left at

a forty-five-degree angle, and scampers ten yards or so across to a room at the far side of the hall. He grabs hold of the door handle and swings it open. "Come on!" he says to us. "What are you waiting for? The coast is clear!"

We're hesitating, because, um, it's only the White House, after all. It just doesn't seem like the right thing to do, to run around the place. Since I'm at the head of the line, I put a foot forward, on the hallway itself, but I do it with about as much confidence as if I'm wading into the ocean in February.

Which Bev, naturally, notices. She gives me a not-so-gentle shove in the back. "Move it, Mel," she says. "Don't be such a scaredy-cat."

"I'm not scared," I say, tiptoeing into the hallway. "I'm *respectful*—get it? There's a difference."

"Sure, Mel," says Bev. "If that works for you, fine." Then Bev and Brandon push behind me and we all stumble forward. We proceed slowly, carefully. There's just something about the place that puts all thoughts of running completely beyond the pale.

Nothing's too fancy, though. There's a very crummy carpet on the floor, for one thing. It might have been golden once, but now it's just brown, dirty brown at that, with a bunch of bald spots and frayed edges. Also, there's hardly anything on the walls—no gilded paintings, no frescoes on the ceilings, nada. The place is plain. And, if I had to say, short on funds.

"Come on!" says Tad. "This is Pa's office. We have to

close the door!" We enter, and we see a desk, chairs, and a medium-sized table in a corner—but other than that, no one's there. "Pa must be in the telegraph office," Tad says. "He goes there all the time, especially when fightin's going on. But we can stay here for a while if you want. You like to sit in Pa's chair? He don't mind, honest!" To demonstrate, Tad goes behind the desk and climbs into what is presumably his father's chair. "Pa lets me sit here any time I want, and I get to make all kinds of important decisions! Why, just the other day I ordered twenty spies to be hanged! I looked at ol' Secretary of War Stanton right in the eye, and I said, 'Now, you see here, Mr. Stanton, we got no business going soft on these Reb spies. I order you to hang 'em all, before the sun sets—or else!'"

"Or else what?" comes an adult voice from behind us. A man, a young man, perhaps in his early twenties, walks into the office from a side door. "Allow me to introduce myself," he says. "I am John Hay, secretary to the president. Tad . . . you were saying?"

Tad barely blinks. "I was sayin', Mr. Hay, that ol' Secretary of War can go find himself a new job! I don't have much use for him anyway. He's always yelling and mean to folks, sometimes even to Pa. I ain't never seen him so much as smile."

"Tad, now who are these fine young friends of yours? And why in heaven's name—if I may ask—are they dressed so strange?" He walks up to me and puts his hand on my shirt. He's not a tall man. He has a very thin mustache, and his somewhat long and shaggy black hair is slicked back across his head. He's wearing a very formal-looking black suit: pants, a jacket that hangs down to his thighs, and a black bow tie. I get the feeling it won't be easy to trick a guy who's smart enough to be a secretary to a president, but it doesn't mean I can't try.

"We come from up north," I say, which doesn't help at all.

"North? As in the North Pole?"

"Ha. No, not that far north."

"How far, then? Maine?"

"No. New Jersey."

"New Jersey? Interesting." Mr. Hay proceeds to examine us more closely. "Tad," he says, "what are your friends' names? And why have I never had the pleasure of meeting them before now?"

It's a good thing—for us—that young Tad can't focus too long on any one thing. He gets off Pa's chair and bolts out of the office. "Come on, everyone!" he shouts. "Let's go on over to the telegraph office and visit Pa!"

"You can't!" shouts Mr. Hay, but it's already too late. Tad has run across the office and out the door, and we're right behind him.

# NINE

ALL OF US, INCLUDING Mr. Hay, run down the stairs, through a hallway, out the front door of the White House, and across the White House lawn.

"Hurry!" yells Tad.

"Stop!" yells Mr. Hay.

Tad leads us to the building directly next to the White House, a large four-story edifice with a bunch of huge columns supporting a portico. There are many more people standing around in front of this building than there are at the White House, but no one seems to be disturbed or surprised by the sight of four kids and one man running across the lawn, up to the front of the building, and then inside.

We run straight up to the second floor. Tad flings open the door to a room on the left side and we fall in at once.

There are five men in the room, which seems to have been, at one time or another, a library. Of the five men, four are young. They are dressed in military uniforms, and each is holding papers in their hands.

One of these young men is sitting in front of a black device, which is on a marble-topped table. This must be the telegraph set.

And seated very close by to the telegraph operator is a tall man, judging by how high he sits in his chair.

The man is pale white, and has a beard but no mustache.

President Abe Lincoln.

Bev, Brandon, and I stop totally dead.

I mean, come on, wouldn't you? Abe Lincoln? *The* Abe Lincoln? He's like three feet away. I haven't felt this awestruck since I first saw General George Washington, alive and atop his great white steed.

"Pa!" says Tad, and runs directly into his dad's arms.

And Pa—that is, President Abe Lincoln—picks him up. "Why, old Tad," he says. "Now you've brought some new friends and I'm afraid we haven't been properly introduced." He puts Tad down, stands up, takes a couple of steps toward us, and thrusts out his large—very large—right hand.

"I'm Mel," I say, and shake his hand. "I'm from New Jersey."

"I'm Beverly," Bev says. "I'm from California."

"And I'm Brandon," Brandon says. "I'm from New Mexico. I mean the territory."

"New Mexico!" says President Lincoln. "Now there's a place I've never been but surely would like to go. Tell me, Brandon, what brings you from the Territory of New Mexico to Washington City?"

It's a question Brandon can't answer, and, thankfully, doesn't have to. A large imposing man with a full beard, a loud voice, and a gruff manner enters the telegraph office.

"There is too much noise in this room!" he says. "Gentlemen, may I remind you that we have a battle of some significance being waged as I speak. Who has read the latest dispatches?"

I happen to know—because, according to Bev, I'm such a history nerd—that a "dispatch" is what they call the reports coming from the telegraph operator. He writes the incoming message on his dispatch pad, then tears them off one by one. "I have them all right here, Secretary Stanton," President Lincoln says, waving a sheaf of papers in his left hand. "But first I was greeting Tad's young friends."

"Mr. President," says Secretary Stanton very wearily. "If you please. May I have the dispatches?"

"I shall review them first," President Lincoln says, and looks at us and winks. He seems to delight in getting Secretary Stanton boiling mad.

"All right," President Lincoln says, reading the first page. "Nothing much here." He flips through the sheaves, nodding his head, then he hands the stack over to Secretary Stanton, who doesn't find anything he likes either.

"Mr. President, really, I must insist," says Secretary Stanton. "These children—all these children—must leave at once. It appears a battle is imminent, Mr. President. We might be called upon to render assistance at any moment."

"Certainly, certainly, I will attend to it, as shall we all. Now, Tad, let me ask you and your young friends to move along now. We've important business."

"A battle, Pa? Where is it this time?"

"Pennsylvania, I'm afraid. General Lee has brought the Confederate Army into the heart of the Union. And they have, by some accounts, encountered our own army. At a little town called Gettysburg."

Touch us all with an electric wire.

*Gettysburg.*

Of course.

It makes perfect sense.

If you were the president and founder of a company called Things Go Wrong, Incorporated, what better place to see to it that things *do* go wrong than right in the middle of the Battle of Gettysburg?

The only mystery now is why it took us so long to figure it out. Why else were we transported back to July 1, 1863?

Make it two mysteries. Why are we in Washington when we should be in a small town in Pennsylvania?

"We'll lick 'em, Pa," Tad says. "Don't you worry 'bout a thing. We'll beat old General Lee like a drum and send him right back where he came from."

President Lincoln raises his eyebrows. "I surely hope so, Tad," he says. "I surely hope so. The alternative is not something I think I can bear to contemplate."

"The alternative, Mr. President," says Secretary of War Stanton, "is that General Lee beats *us* like a drum. And then he shall be able to march unimpeded to Washington City from the north. At which point we would not only have no army, but no defense. We have a need to formulate contingency plans, Mr. President. Should the worst happen. Now—perhaps Tad and his friends would like to run along. Before they learn any more military secrets."

"Secrets? I doubt there are any, Mr. Secretary. I've looked through the telegrams. I'd venture a guess that no one is entirely certain what is going on."

"Mr. President?" I say.

"Yes, son?"

"I think things will work out just fine. Just so long as no one *interferes* with anything."

"Interfere? With a battle? I'm afraid many will try, son. They are called soldiers."

"I don't mean that. I mean *outside* interference."

"Outside of what?"

"Mr. President," says Secretary Stanton, "if you please, sir. I do not think it proper for you to be debating military tactics with this . . . *boy*. Let me send them all on their way. Go now, children. Go and play outside."

"Wait a minute," I say, as Secretary Stanton puts his hand on my shoulder and tries to shove me along. "They might be there already—trying to *interfere* with things."

"Where?" says President Lincoln.

"Don't listen to him, Mr. President," says Secretary Stanton. "I beg of you. I will see to it they leave."

"I know what you're up to," Tad blurts out, looking at me. "You want to go bomb ol' General Lee, I'm dead certain! You want to give him one of them shiny black bombs you carry in your pocket and blow 'em all to smithereens!"

It doesn't take long for everyone in the telegraph office—the four clerks, Secretary Stanton, and President Lincoln—to jump to their feet.

Maybe like a half a millisecond.

Secretary Stanton—who has been coming across as a big, mean, ornery, know-it-all grouch—immediately places himself between us and President Lincoln, shielding his boss from an impending explosion.

The four telegraph operators grab us.

Then they throw us to the floor.

Two take care of Brandon, one takes care of Bev, and one takes care of me.

The guy who takes care of me *really* takes care of me. He's got his knee in the middle of my back.

His arm around my neck.

And one hand pawing every pocket.

It doesn't take him long to find my phone, or the others to find Brandon's and Bev's.

We're hauled to our feet. And thrown against a far wall.

"Leave 'em be!" cries Tad. "Tell 'em to leave 'em be, Pa! They're spies! Working for us! They told me so themselves!"

One of the clerks gathers all three phones and presents them to Secretary Stanton, who points to the nearest window. "Get them out!" Secretary Stanton yells. "Get them out before they blow!"

The clerk runs to the window, which is already open, and heaves them.

Just like that.

Flings our phones as far as he can.

Which means: unless we get them back, we'll never see home again.

Everyone—except Brandon, Bev, and me—then hunches over, puts their hands to their ears, and waits for the sound that will never come.

"Those aren't bombs!" Brandon says. "They're . . . they're toys!"

"You told me they was bombs!" Tad says. "You ain't nothing but a liar if you told me wrong!"

"Mr. President!" Secretary of War Stanton shouts. "Mr. President! We must get these children out of here at once! It is utter chaos!"

Then we hear a loud clacking noise, and the telegraph clerks run to their chairs to get the incoming messages.

"Out!" yells Secretary Stanton. "Out at once, all of you!"

He points. His men grab us by the shoulders and march us to the door. The last thing we see is President Abraham Lincoln, his hands outstretched and open, as if he's utterly powerless to do a thing.

"And stay out!" Secretary Stanton says, before slamming the door to the telegraph office right in our faces.

# TEN

"WE HAVE TO GET our phones!" I yell. "Hurry!"

We start running down the stairs as fast as we can. Tad tags behind, but right now he's the least of our concerns.

We exit the building, bumping into every bystander in our way, then run around the corner and down the side until we are underneath the second-floor window where our "bombs" were tossed.

We see them.

Two black, one white.

On a grassy patch of green. Which saves our necks. Because if they had been tossed out a front window, they would have landed on stone, and that would not have been good.

Our phones, from twenty yards away, seem to be intact. The problem is, we're not the only ones looking at them.

Or wanting them.

A man—not old, not young, but definitely a man—is standing maybe ten yards away from our phones. He's tallish. He's wearing a black jacket, black pants, and a black bowler hat. And he has a big black walrus-style mustache. Around his neck there's a strap. Connected to a leather satchel. Stenciled on the side of the satchel, in big black letters: T.G.W., INC.

We stop. "Hey!" yells Bev. "Back off!"

The guy comes closer. He's now nine yards from our phones.

Tad's in tears. He doesn't seem to understand that we have something else on our mind right at the moment. "You told me you was spies," he says. "You told me!"

"Not now," says Bev. "See that guy? I think he wants our ph—our toys. And he can't have them."

The guy's now eight yards away, and calculating his chances.

"Back off!" Bev yells again.

"You heard her!" chimes in Brandon.

"Those are ours!" Bev says. "Back off, mister—it's your last warning!"

Very slowly the guy unlatches his satchel. I can pretty much guess that there's one thing in there we're not going to want to see.

But those phones?

They're ours. And nobody—nobody but nobody—is going to take them from us a second time. We snatch them off the ground and stuff them in our pockets.

He laughs, and then he reaches into his satchel and pulls something out.

It's not a pistol. It's a *piece of paper*.

"This is for you," he says.

"What is it?" asks Bev

"A message," the guy says.

"From who?" says Brandon.

"I have been hired to deliver this," the man says. "I am employed by the Pinkerton Detective Agency."

"Who hired you?" I say.

"That would be confidential, so never you mind. My instructions are to find the three of you, but you got four. Ain't your name Mel? And ain't hers Beverly and his Brandon? Who's this other one?" He nods his head to Tad.

"My name is Tad Lincoln," Tad says. "And my pa is president of the United States!"

"Well, blow me down," the man says. "And I'm the Prince of Wales. But I ain't gonna stand here much longer. Take the message!"

I reach up and take it.

"Tad!" we hear. "Tad!" Poking his head out of the telegraph office window is President Lincoln, with a big grin on his face. "You take care of those bombs, you hear? Mother will not be pleased if they go off in the house!"

"All right, Pa!" says Tad.

"Well, I'll be darned," says Mr. Walrus Mustache. "Can't say I believed you, about being Tad Lincoln. But it don't change a thing. You read that note, and you heed it. Now I believe I'll be on my way. I expect never to see any of you ever again. If I do, it ain't gonna be so friendly. Mark my words well."

"And who exactly are you again?" Bev says.

"They call me Hubie," the man says. "That's all you need know." Then he tips his hat, turns around, and walks away.

"What a whack job," Brandon says.

"Yeah, but he knows our names," I say. "That's what's really strange."

"How do you know that man?" says Tad.

"We don't," I say. "But somehow he knows us." I unfold the note—typed, not handwritten—and we read it together:

*Children,*

*I will give you this much—you are full of surprises. I admit I did not expect this amount of resourcefulness on your part, but in the end it makes no difference: I will prevail, and you will not. I will concede that your endeavors on behalf of General Washington were lucky in the extreme. But then I had no way of factoring in your actions, or indeed of even knowing of your existence. So score one point for your side. I am quite certain it will be your last.*

*My activities are far too profound to warrant an explanation to any of you, but let it be said I make no pretense as to my intentions, and never have. The good Professor Moncrieff hides his wiles behind a façade of respectability. I do not. Nevertheless, you would be well advised to return—immediately—to that basement headquarters from which you came. Perhaps you can direct your energies unto Professor Moncrieff, if you still retain any lingering taste for adventure. Or you can return docilely to your school and continue your holiday until the new term begins. Soon enough all of this will fade from your memory as you return to your school-day routine. The choice is yours.*

*But you may linger here no longer. Consider this your one and only warning. From this moment henceforth you will be considered enemy combatants. And, as such, you will be considered armed, dangerous, and an eminently suitable target for termination of the most prejudicial variety.*

*One last item: nothing, thanks to me, remains the same, neither in the present nor the past. Do not presume that the app on your phones remains the same. I have had "time," you see, to amend things.*

*And as time itself is my plaything, I bequeath to you a small allotment. Sufficient "time"—as you understand the meaning of the word—to reprogram your phones and return home. But you must act immediately. If you refuse to exercise this most generous of offers, you will be very, very sorry. You will not, however, have long to endure your regrets.*

*Kurtis*
*President, T.G.W., Inc.*

"He's trying to scare us away," I say. "Somehow he knows we're here this time."

"It's sort of working," Brandon says. "What does 'termination of the most prejudicial variety' mean?"

"I don't think it means anything good," I say.

"So what are we going to do?" says Bev. "Be scared off?"

"Not me," I say.

"Me neither," says Bev. "Brandon?"

Brandon shakes his head no. "I'm not scared off, but what's the plan?"

"I think our plan ought to be to make a plan," I say.

"That helps, Mel," says Brandon. "Like, not at all."

"Don't be *useless*, Mel," says Bev. "You're the one who's supposed to know so much. If today's the Battle of Gettysburg, and we're here in Washington, then it's already too late, isn't it? For us to do anything about it?"

"No. The Battle of Gettysburg took three days. July first, second, and third. It wasn't decided until the third day."

"And how come you know so much again?" says Brandon.

"The History Channel. I used to watch it all the time with my dad."

"So are you spies or ain't you?" Tad says. "And are them things bombs or are they toys? You got a habit of sayin' one thing and meanin' the other. I ain't done with you yet. I can march right back to ol' Secretary Stanton and have him arrest you all on account of treason and lyin'."

"We are spies," Bev says. "But we're so top secret not even Secretary Stanton knows about it. Super top secret."

"Does Pa know?"

"Of course he does. But he can't let on. Especially not with all the telegraphs clerks hanging around. It's for their own good."

"Really?" Tad asks.

"Really," I say. Before I can elaborate, someone very tall, with very large hands, clomps Tad on the shoulder and grins at us.

"Tad," says President Abraham Lincoln, "I think we ought to invite your new friends to stay for dinner. Lord knows we haven't heard the sounds of happy children in quite a while. It might do poor Mother some good. But they might be advised to . . . ah . . . clean up a bit around the edges. Tad, show them the way to the washroom. My young friends, do we have a deal?"

Tad's face lights up; the president of the United States grins. The rest is up to us.

Brandon and I are struck dumb, so it's up to Bev to do the honors.

"We'd be delighted to have dinner with you, sir," Bev says. "It would be a thrill of a lifetime."

"Come on, then!" yells Tad, and starts running into the White House. "What are you all waitin' for?"

**WHITE HOUSE GUESTS AND GHOSTS**

# ELEVEN

A T SEVEN P.M., IN Mr. Lincoln's White House, dinner is served. We cleaned up the best we could, and we're sitting in the Family Dining Room on the first floor. President Lincoln is at one end of the table, and Mrs. Lincoln is at the other. Bev and I are on one side; Brandon and Tad are on the other.

The room is way more homey than fancy—not what I expected, this being the White House and all. There's the dining room table and chairs, and a sideboard along one wall, but that's pretty much it. Another worn carpet, some very old wallpaper, but no paintings or other decorations. Good enough for the family, I guess, but not a place to invite a king or queen.

Mrs. Lincoln looks at me. "You," she says, "are sitting

exactly where Willie sat." There is no doubt, by the tone of her voice, that this makes her unhappy. "I thought this seat was not to be taken," she says to the president. "Why is it?"

The president of the United States shrugs, then frowns. "We have guests, Mother," he says. "I thought enough time has ... er ... passed ... from the one thing to the other. . . ."

"Whatever are you trying to say, Father?" Mrs. Lincoln snaps. "This seat has been vacant a year. Now it is filled. No one asked *me* what I thought about it. And by the very child who nearly caused my death this afternoon! Honestly. I know not how you think at times."

"He explained himself, Mother. An accident, merely an accident. A case of the wrong person being in the wrong place. Which reminds me of a time I was on the legal circuit in Illinois . . ."

"I'm not in the mood for one of your stories," Mrs. Lincoln says. "Now say grace and let's eat."

We bow our heads, and the president thanks the Lord for dinner. He also asks for a blessing, for the good men at Gettysburg.

"Gettysburg?" Mrs. Lincoln asks. "Wherever is that?"

"It's in Pennsylvania, Ma," says Tad. "We just learned today, General Lee brought his Confederate Army up there, and they're going to have it out once and for all with the Union Army. Ain't that right, Pa?"

"We'll see, son," President Lincoln says. "Now, where are those potatoes?"

"Who we got leading our men this time, Pa?" Tad asks. "Who'd you put in charge of the Union Army? General Hooker? I like him. Fightin' Joe Hooker. He'll see to it ol' General Lee gets the lickin' he deserves!"

"No, Tad, it won't be General Hooker this time," says President Lincoln. "It'll be General Meade. He's a fine man, Tad. A fine man indeed."

"General Meade? Pa, I never heard of 'im! Since when has he been made in charge of the Union Army?"

"Well, let's see now. Today is Wednesday. I guess it was Sunday, we made it official."

"Sunday? Pa, you mean to say you put this General Meade in charge of the whole entire Union Army three days ago? Pa! How could you?"

"Well, Tad, if you must know, General Hooker up and resigned the post. Not that we were so sorry to see him go. You know how it's been with my generals, son. Other than General Grant, I can't seem to find any who seem to want to *fight*. They do like to organize, and order supplies, and parade, but they just never seem to get to the fighting part of the equation, when that is plainly what is called for. But I do not think General Meade will be able to avoid the thing itself this time, though. General Lee will force a fight upon him, whether he wishes it or no. How this goes, right now none can say. I'm afraid the information we're getting from the field is inconclusive. Highly inconclusive."

"Enough of this war talk, Father," says Mrs. Lincoln.

"Now, are we going to eat, or are we going to discuss military strategy?"

A thin, bald, oldish butler, who is called Mr. Goodchild, starts to bring in one dish after the other, but instead of serving each one of us he gives the dish to President Lincoln, who takes a portion and then passes the dish around the table. First are the potatoes, then green beans, then biscuits, and finally chicken in a cream gravy, which, according to Tad, is the president's favorite. Everyone takes modest portions, except Mrs. Lincoln, who serves herself heaps of everything.

"So tell us, young miss," Mrs. Lincoln says. "Do you attend a school for young ladies, perhaps? Are you learning all the tender household arts? And these clothes of yours—I must say, I have held my tongue, but have you not a proper dress?"

"I don't, ma'am," Bev says. "Not with me, anyway." Bev is going to be a brain surgeon someday, remember. For newborns. That, *and* find the cure for cancer. Fashion, so far as I know, is not high on her list of priorities.

"Now, dear, I'm sure we could come up with something, couldn't we? Mrs. Keckley!" Mrs. Lincoln shouts. "Somebody get me Mrs. Keckley!"

Mr. Goodchild, who up till now hasn't said a word, speaks. "Shall I find her for you, ma'am?"

"Of course you shall!" Mrs. Lincoln says. "Tell her to come at once. This young lady is in need of a dress."

"I don't think that will be necessary," Bev says. "We'll be on our way soon, after all. No reason to bother."

"Pshaw," Mrs. Lincoln says. "Child, I have no daughter, but I was young once, and what I would have given for a brand-new dress! It's decided. You shall have one. Mrs. Keckley! What is taking so long?"

Mr. Goodchild, who hasn't even had a chance yet to leave the room to locate Mrs. Keckley, mutters something under his breath, and shuffles out of the dining room, but not in any particular hurry.

"And where might you be on your way to?" President Lincoln says to Bev. "If you don't mind my asking. With all these soldiers about at night—well, even I have heard stories about Washington City. Though everyone does make such an effort to protect me from learning about such unpleasantness. Of which, I assure you, I have had my full share. Why, I think it was perhaps twenty years ago, and this is in a most remote part of Illinois, barely a stone's toss from Missouri, where I was called upon to investigate a murder most—"

"Abraham!" interrupts Mrs. Lincoln. "If you please, this is dinner, and children are present! I will not have one of your sordid stories besmirching our table. Now, where is she? Mrs. Keckley! What does one have to do around this abominable place to get an answer! Mrs. Keckley!"

"No reason to raise your voice, Mother," says the president.

"I shall raise my voice if I please!" says Mrs. Lincoln. "This girl is dressed in little more than rags—boy's clothes, I dare say—and since no one else seems prepared to do something about it, I will! Mrs. Keckley! Get down here at once and make this girl a dress! A gingham dress, in blue!"

"I really, really don't think that's necessary," Bev says.

"You don't like blue? We could make it in green if you'd rather!"

"Pa, I think you're right," says Tad. "They shouldn't be wandering round Washington City at night. They should stay here with us, at least for the night. Can they, Pa, can they?"

Before he can answer, there is a knock on the door. It's not Mrs. Keckley. It's Mr. Hay, President Lincoln's secretary. "Mr. President," he says, "Secretary Stanton begs you to come at once to the telegraph office. There is news from Gettysburg. General Reynolds has been killed, and General Meade is not yet upon the field."

"Oh dear," says President Lincoln. "That does not bode well. Excuse me, everyone." And with that, the president and Mr. Hay leave us, while Mrs. Lincoln and Bev are still staring each other down. Both of them look like they're about ready to explode.

Before that happens—before *anything* happens—the now famous Mrs. Keckley enters, followed closely by Mr. Goodchild.

"Mrs. Keckley," Mr. Goodchild grandly announces.

"Well, I can see that with my own two eyes, can't I?" snarls Mrs. Lincoln. "Honestly. Mrs. Keckley, would you be so kind? This girl is in dire need. Of a dress. Can you come up something? Now, perhaps?"

"Now, Mrs. Lincoln?" says Mrs. Keckley. She seems to be a very kindly woman, but stressed by the request. "I would need a half day at least. I'd have to take the child's measurements. . . ."

"No time for that." Mrs. Lincoln waves her hand. "We are going to the Red Room shortly, and I wish the girl to be . . . to have a dress. What she is wearing now simply won't do. Fix something up—take something of mine—I don't care what you do—but get this girl in a dress! You have one hour, Mrs. Keckley. I don't want to hear any more about it. Off with you then. The both of you. Come down to the Red Room in one hour."

"But, Mrs. Lincoln . . . ," Bev says. "We really have to be going. We have . . . we have an appointment!"

"An appointment? At this hour? I think not! You have just been invited to *the* Red Room, young lady, by the wife of the president of the United States! Have you any idea how coveted an invitation this is? Now be off with you, before I change my mind. Take her, Mrs. Keckley! Take her away and fix her!"

Bev has no choice, and allows herself to be escorted from the dining room by Mrs. Keckley, not without first giving Brandon and me dagger stares. After she's gone, Mr. Goodchild begins removing our plates and silverware, but Mrs. Lincoln slaps the table.

"Enough!" Mrs. Lincoln says. "There's no time! Summon Lord Colchester!"

"Lord Colchester, ma'am?" says Mr. Goodchild. "Are

you quite sure? I was under the impression that . . . after that last time . . . when . . . the exposure . . . of the apparatus . . ."

"Did I ask for your opinion, Mr. Goodchild? I said, summon Lord Colchester! You are not to question me! Summon him, I tell you. I must have him here within the hour. And prepare the Red Room! We shall have our gathering!"

"Ma'am," Mr. Goodchild says, quickly moving away from the table so he is out of whacking range of the First Lady, "Mr. Lincoln said, he told me himself, that if he ever so much as catches scent of Lord Colchester, let alone sees him, he will order an entire brigade to hog-tie him to the nearest horse post. Told me that not the other day, ma'am, swear he did."

"If you value your position," Mrs. Lincoln says coldly, "then you will do as I ask. This one here," she says, pointing her short right finger at Brandon, "he speaks!"

"He's hardly said a word, beg pardon," says Mr. Goodchild.

"He speaks to the spirits!" cries Mrs. Lincoln.

"I do?" says Brandon.

"You do!" says Mrs. Lincoln. "And you have far, far more to tell us—I can feel it in my bones! You can tell us of the past—and you can predict the future!"

"I can?" says Brandon.

"Of course you can, child," Mrs. Lincoln says, and puts her hand on Brandon's hand. "We only need the peculiar genius of Lord Colchester to reach into your very depths and bring it to the light, so all the world will know! You will tell us of Willie—you will speak to him—you will *commune* with him—you will let Willie know he is not alone!"

"I will?" says Brandon.

"You will, my child, you will! To the Red Room in one hour, everyone! Make sure Lord Colchester arrives!"

# TWELVE

AN HOUR LATER BRANDON and me—but not Tad—are herded into the Red Room. Tad, we gather, is too young and vulnerable to be allowed to participate. They must call it the Red Room because of the deep red carpet. But it's also way fancier than any other room we've seen at the White House. There's a grand piano, gold molding, vases, even a huge portrait of my old pal General George Washington.

A round table is in the middle of the room, surrounded by seven straight-backed chairs. A red tablecloth covers the table. Mr. Goodchild nods to Brandon and me to take our seats. We're left alone for a few minutes before Bev makes a royal entrance. She's followed by Mrs. Keckley, and neither of them seems happy in the least. Bev is wearing a dress, though. It's not blue, it's not green, and it's not gingham, but it is a dress. Yellow, with sleeves. And a frilly white collar.

"Don't say a word," she says, taking her seat. "Neither one of you. Or else I'll let you have it."

We don't have a chance to say a word, because Mr. Goodchild swings open the door and shouts, "The First Lady of the United States!" He motions at us with his hand, and we rise to our feet. Into the room comes Mrs. Lincoln, regal as a queen. She's changed her clothes too—she's wearing a rich purple dress now, with a pearl necklace, and she's also put her hair up. In her left hand she holds a fan. Mr. Goodchild pulls her chair out and helps her get seated.

"Sit, Mrs. Keckley," Mrs. Lincoln says. "We mustn't have an even number. It is one of the rules, I'm afraid."

"Must I, ma'am?" says Mrs. Keckley. "I have so much work to do. . . ."

"You must," says Mrs. Lincoln. "Sit down next to the girl. Make sure she sits up."

Bev shoots Brandon and me another glare. Then we hear a commotion in the hallway outside the Red Room, and a furious voice roars: "Unhand me, I say! I am Lord Colchester, and the First Lady has requested my presence!"

We hear the sounds of a scuffle. Mr. Goodchild exits to see what is going on, and then, a minute later, he opens the door and announces the guest: "Ladies and gentlemen—Lord Charles J. Colchester!"

Everyone stands except Mrs. Lincoln as Lord

Colchester—short, dapper, slicked-back hair, dressed very formally—enters the Red Room. "My dear madam," he says in a most posh English accent. He bows to Mrs. Lincoln, takes her hand and kisses it. "My dear, most dear, madam. The spirits are very strong this night, very strong indeed! I feel we are on the cusp of something . . . something most profound!

"But silence! I sense the spirits before we start! Most curious, most curious indeed. No one move!"

No one does. Lord Colchester proceeds to circle our table, his hand outstretched, as if he's afraid to bump into something solid. Then he walks around the room, his hands still outstretched, until he is apparently satisfied. "Everyone, be seated," he says, looking at the butler, Mr. Goodchild, who sits down next to Brandon and me. "We must start immediately. The spirits are eager to communicate with us!"

Lord Colchester circles our table again, this time with his hands hovering a second or two above each person's head. As he does this he mumbles something—in Latin maybe, or Greek—before moving on to the next person. When he puts his hands over Bev's head, he pulls back for an instant, as if he's just touched something hot. Bev frowns, and glares at me, as if *I've* done something wrong.

Then Lord Colchester comes to Brandon. His hands shake at first, he's so excited. "My word!" he says. "What have we here?"

"What is it, Lord Colchester?" asks Mrs. Lincoln. "What is it?"

"A most unusual . . . a very strong signal . . . a veritable conducting medium . . . I say, who is this lad? How has he come to be in this house?"

"I knew it!" cries Mrs. Lincoln. "I touched him myself, with my own hands—he has the gift! He communes with the dead!"

"No, I really can't do that," says Brandon. "I don't even *want* to do that. . . ."

"Silence!" commands Lord Colchester. "We must have silence, I insist upon it! Or else the spirits will not come!"

He moves over to me, puts his hands above my head—maybe an inch or so away—and I can actually *feel* the heat of his hands. "Hmm," he says. "Nothing much here. Mr. Goodchild, if you please: time to prepare the table."

Mr. Goodchild gets up, and a moment later returns with three white candles, a glass of milk, and a hunk of bread. He lights the candles, turns down the gas lamps in the room, and returns to his seat. Mrs. Lincoln lays on the table a framed black-and-white photograph of a boy—Willie Lincoln, I assume.

"Let us join hands," Lord Colchester says. His voice has gotten very low, and very spooky. The Red Room is big, with high ceilings, and the candles cast a glow over everyone's faces, which adds to the overall effect. With my right hand I clasp on to Mr. Goodchild's hand, and with my left hand I take hold of Lord Colchester's. There is a difference—a *big* difference—in each man's hand. Mr. Goodchild's is small, warm, and clammy; Lord Colchester's is large, cold, and kind of rubbery or something.

"Spirits of the past," Lord Colchester intones. "We are gathered here in this room, on this first day of July, to summon you. Move among us if you will. Be guided by the light of this world and visit upon us. Everyone, repeat with me: 'Be guided by the light of this world. Visit upon us.'"

"Be guided by the light of this world," we all repeat, as slowly and as mournfully as we can. "Visit upon us."

"Beloved Willie, son of Abraham and Mary, we bring you gifts from life unto death. Be guided by the light of this world and visit upon us."

It's our cue, and so we repeat: "Be guided by the light of this world and visit upon us."

"Dearest Willie, I am Lord Colchester, your medium and guide from one world to the next. Through me you can communicate, through the ether and through the mists, to your loving mother, Mary, faithful wife of Abraham, and to all who gather here this night. We are believers, dearest Willie, in life and in death; all are one, boundaries are none. Speak with us! If you hear us, Willie, send us a signal! Let us hear your presence!"

We then hear—and I am not kidding—a soft thumping, almost like a tom-tom drum. But slow, steady— *thump, thump, thump.* Then the very faint jingle of a bell.

"Let us know it is you, dearest Willie. We have brought you milk and bread, for sustenance from one world to the next. Tap once for yes, twice for no. Is it you, Willie? Is it you, Willie Lincoln, son of Abraham and Mary?"

The bells jingle a little louder, rising to a crescendo, and then stop. Mrs. Lincoln gasps.

Then we hear, plain as day, one distinct tap, like a soft knock on a door.

"Behold!" says Lord Colchester. "Willie has come to us!"

"Willie!" says Mrs. Lincoln. "Is it you?"

Another soft tap. Like on a door. Or underneath the table. I can feel Mr. Goodchild squeezing my hand each time the bell jingles, but Lord Colchester's hand never varies in pressure, or in warmth, or in any other way. But before I can think it through, the table starts to shake, like it's attempting to rise up.

Mr. Goodchild squeezes my hand so tight it hurts.

"It is Willie, son of Abraham and Mary!" says Lord Colchester. "He comes to us at last! Speak, oh, Willie, speak to us through me, your humble and obedient servant. Are you well?"

Two taps. Mrs. Lincoln nearly falls from her chair. "My God!" she says. "I knew something was wrong!" She turns to Brandon. "Speak to him! Do something!"

"I'm not sure I—" Brandon begins.

"Silence!" says Lord Colchester. "Only I am able to speak with Willie! Only I!"

"Ask Willie what's wrong!" Mrs. Lincoln says. "Ask him, what can we do to help?"

"I remind you, dear madam, that each question must

be framed for a positive or negative response. One tap for yes, two taps for—"

"I know, I know! You need not spell it out, Lord Colchester, I quite remember. Willie, it is your mother, your loving mother: is there anything we can do?"

Two taps for no. Two distinct taps, which come from either underneath the table or from the beyond.

"We miss you so terribly, Willie," Mrs. Lincoln says. "Are you lonely where you are? Do you miss us?"

One tap.

"He misses us!" says Mrs. Lincoln. "Poor Willie! I knew he would come tonight! Willie, my dear boy, do you wish to join us? In person?"

Two taps.

"No? Why on earth not? Willie, are you sure?"

One tap.

"Willie, I am your mother. Join us, join us right now! Through this lad—Brandon is his name—join us, I beg you!"

"Mrs. Lincoln," says Lord Colchester, "please be most careful! If you anger the spirits, they will leave us and they may never return! It is only with the greatest difficulty they are able to journey from their world to ours. It is most demanding, most exhausting . . . I fear we are losing our connection!"

"We must not!" Mrs. Lincoln says. "We need to ask if he can see into the future. Can you guide us? Your dear father can use every last bit of help, every last bit! Can you, Willie, can you?"

A single tap is the response.

"Oh my word!" says Mrs. Keckley.

"Impossible!" says Mr. Goodchild.

"Silence!" says Lord Colchester. "Mrs. Lincoln, I assure you Willie can travel in worlds that are yet to be, as well as from the otherworld. Ask, madam, ask him anything, and he shall be compelled to tell you the truth!"

"I have a question," comes a voice, from behind us. Not a voice sitting at our round table, holding hands, but a familiar voice nonetheless. "Shall we prevail at Gettysburg? It is really the only question any of us should be asking. For I fear the future of the Republic depends upon it."

None of us break the circle, or unclasp our hands, but all of us turn our heads to the rear of the Red Room. There, his face barely visible in the flickering candles from our table, is President Lincoln.

# THIRTEEN

"LIGHT, I BEG," THE president says. "It is already too dark. I fear it may get darker still. Mr. Hay? If you please."

Mr. Hay goes to the nearest gas lamp and turns the knob, and in seconds the room brightens. He goes to a second and third lamp and repeats the process. The Red Room is now alight and in full glory.

The president lowers himself into the nearest chair, right by the door. No one mentions that our séance has just been disrupted, least of all Lord Colchester, who is fumbling with something on his lap. I see, before he puts everything away, a fake rubber hand, a small drum, and a bracelet with little bells upon it.

There can be no doubt as to what we've been doing, but the president seems preoccupied with other things.

I have the impression this isn't the first time he's caught his wife conducting a séance, but that it doesn't particularly upset him.

"Have you ill news, Father?" says Mrs. Lincoln. She too, it appears, will say nothing about the séance, or about the round table we're sitting at, or the still-lit candles, or the strange personage who goes by the name of "Lord" Colchester.

"Ill news? General Reynolds has been slain, but that we've known. He commanded the army's First Corps. I had asked him to command the entire Union Army, but he made his acceptance contingent upon certain preconditions, preconditions I could not, alas, accept. And so I chose instead General Meade. Now Reynolds is dead, but it appears he has, nonetheless, committed us to battle. I have been in the telegraph office waiting for word on how the battle goes. We have heard nothing. The worst may have already happened, or may be happening as we speak. You, sir," the president says, nodding his head at Lord Colchester, "claim to speak with the dead. And did I not just hear you say that the dead are able to travel in worlds that are yet to be? Ask then. Who shall prevail at Gettysburg? Has our army already been defeated?"

"They haven't been!" Brandon blurts out. "It's just beginning!"

"I knew it!" Mrs. Lincoln says. "He has powers, this one! Willie, is it you? Have you descended upon this boy in order to speak to us?"

"Mother, I don't believe anyone has or is able to descend upon anyone else," says the president. "But you speak with certainty, young fellow. How so?"

"Well," Brandon says, "I don't really *know* anything. I just *feel* it. Right, Mel? The battle isn't over yet, is it?"

"I don't think it is," I say. "It's night. Things will probably start up tomorrow. I suppose."

If the president has any hesitation about talking military strategy with us civilians, it doesn't show. "General Meade has not yet arrived upon the battlefield, if indeed this is the battlefield," he says. "We have no sense—Secretary Stanton and I—how the troops have been deployed, or indeed, even whether all the troops are acting in unison. They could be scattered throughout Pennsylvania, for all we know, not concentrated at the point of battle. It is most exasperating not to know full well exactly what is going on. Most exasperating indeed. Lack of knowledge at such a time produces in us impotent seething, but little else of value. If only I could think of something!"

Lord Colchester stands up. "Well, I must be going. Very good of you, madam, to have invited me. I can see myself out."

"Wait," says Mr. Hay. "Were you not told not to come back? You, sir, are a fraud and a charlatan. You prey upon the bereaved. You must leave Washington City at once or you shall be arrested for swindling and connivance!"

"Calm yourself, Mr. Hay, calm yourself," says President Lincoln. "We needn't expend the energy on such a minor matter. Leave us now, sir, and spare us any more of your efforts. It is not the dead with whom I wish to communicate; it is the living."

Lord Colchester, seeing his chance, slides over to the door and slithers away. Mr. Goodchild stands up and begins fussing around, as if he had been engaged all along in a useful activity, and not attending a séance.

"I do not dismiss it entirely," the president says. "Although I am as capable as any man in spotting a cheat. I have had dreams that have been portents, Mother, you know I have. I have had strong, powerfully strong impressions that have borne the fruit of bitter reality. And now I have the very real sense that something crooked is afoot. I feel like I am at a poker table, and the cards are not being dealt fairly. I cannot as of yet prove it. But I sense it. There are forces at work that wish to deprive us of what ought to be ours. You, lad, from the New Mexico Territory—your name again?"

"Brandon," says Brandon.

"Brandon. You seemed, just now, positively certain that the battle at Gettysburg is not yet lost. I watched your face as you spoke. I have been in many a court of law, and I have represented, if the truth be told, far more the guilty than the innocent. I have had folk look me dead in the eye and say up is down and black is white. After a good many years, one learns quickly—if one wishes to remain in the practice—how to determine if what a person says is strictly confined to the field of the true, or if there is straying to the field of the untrue. It is not difficult, I think, to tell rather quickly in which field Lord Colchester dwells. But you, Brandon, you speak the truth as you know it, do you not? You speak not as if you are wishing, or guessing, but as if you know. And so I ask a most simple question: how could you know?"

Brandon's about ready to open his mouth, when the door flings open and little Tad Lincoln flies into the Red Room.

"Ghosts!" he cries. "Ma, Pa—ghosts! Upstairs! I heard 'em! They woke me up!" Then he rushes headlong into his father's lap and starts bawling his head off.

And when Tad bawls, he really *bawls*. There is no way for anyone else to say a *word*. He has everyone's complete and undivided attention, which I guess is what he was after in the first place.

Mrs. Lincoln rushes over to comfort Tad, as do Mrs. Keckley, Mr. Hay, and Mr. Goodchild. "There's ghosts— I swear!" cried Tad. "I heard 'em! They're upstairs in the attic! They're planning on something, Pa, I swear, no tellin' what it might be! We got to stop 'em before it's too late!"

"Now, son, I'm sure there's no ghosts. Mice maybe. But no ghosts."

"There are, Pa, there are! I heard 'em!"

"Well, why don't we go on up and see for ourselves. Now, Tad, I'm not afraid of ghosts, but I am afraid of mice. So you'll need to protect me when we go up—is it a deal?"

"Sure it is, Pa. Ma? Will you come with us? And how about them?" Tad says, pointing to Brandon, Bev, and me. "We need all the help we can get!"

# FOURTEEN

"**W**E'LL ALL GO," THE president says. And so we march out of the Red Room, climb the stairs to the second floor, and then climb the stairs to the attic. President Lincoln is carrying Tad, and Mrs. Lincoln is right behind them. Then Mr. Hay, Mrs. Keckley, Mr. Goodchild, Bev, Brandon, and me, last in line.

Mr. Hay is holding a gas lantern, which provides the only light. We see some trunks. Some chairs and tables.

The floorboards creak beneath our feet.

Mrs. Lincoln grabs Brandon's hand.

"They're hidin'," Tad says. "They heard us comin' and they hid!"

"Maybe so, Tad, maybe so," says President Lincoln. "Reminds me of the time this old farmer claimed ghosts burned down his barn. Seems as if the old fellow—"

"Enough of that, Father," says Mrs. Lincoln. But her voice is shaky, and I notice her free hand—the one not latched on to Brandon's—trembling. "Tad, as you can plainly see, there are no ghosts in the attic. Now, I don't know about everyone else, but I'm exhausted. There's been entirely too much commotion this day. Tad, we are going to get you to bed, and no more ghosts will you see or hear tonight. Do you understand me?"

"Yes, Ma," Tad says. "But I swear I heard 'em. I swear!"

"Certainly you might have, Tad. We've all been under such pressure. Father, everyone to bed now. And children—I'm afraid I haven't asked. Where are you staying—at a hotel?"

"Um, yeah, that's right," Bev says. "A hotel."

"Which one?"

"Which one? Why, the uh . . . the uh . . . the big one. Downtown."

"Do you mean Willard's?"

"Yes, that's it. Willard's."

"How in the world can you children afford Willard's? It's by far the most expensive hotel in Washington City!"

Before Bev can answer, we hear something, in the farthest, darkest corner of the attic. It sounds very much like a groan.

The president raises his hand, commanding us to silence. The tiny hairs on the back of my neck start to tingle, and I don't even believe in ghosts.

Or I didn't think I did. We wait, silent, all of us, staring into the far dark corner. Then Mrs. Keckley, the dressmaker—the last person I expected to break the silence—lets out a gasp.

"I think I saw something move!" she whispers.

Mrs. Lincoln's free hand flies to her mouth.

"I saw it too!" cries Tad. "A ghost! You see, Pa? I wasn't lyin', I swear I wasn't!"

"No one said as much, Tad," the president says. He too—if you want to know the truth—seems to be a little, well, *nervous*. Which is a nicer word to use than *scared*, especially when we're talking about the president of the United States, who everyone knows is not supposed to be scared of anything.

"I shall take care of this," Mr. Hay says. "Please wait here. I will shine my lantern on that corner and prove that nothing is there. Certainly not a ghost."

"I beg you be careful, John," the president says. "Have you . . . the right equipment? Upon your person?"

"I have no weapon, sir, if that is what you mean," Mr. Hay says, moving forward. "But I shall not need one, I am sure of it. Our imaginations have gotten the better of us, I'm afraid."

And then we hear—and this time no mistake—a long, low, trilling . . . giggle? A horse whinny? Something for sure, though. Even the brave Mr. Hay stops in his tracks.

"It's the evil spirit!" Mrs. Lincoln sobs. "I knew this house was haunted, I swear I did!"

Then the . . . the evil spirit, or dog-sized horse, does move. We see a shadow flicker across the wall, and then that sinister trilling whinny again.

"Father!" cries Mrs. Lincoln. "Do something!"

But it's Tad who does something. He wrestles himself free of his father's grip, lands on his feet, dodges past Mr. Hay, and dashes toward the shadow. "Tad!" shout the president and Mr. Hay in unison. "Tad!"

"I'll get it!" Tad says.

"Oh my word, I am petrified!" Mrs. Lincoln screams, falling backward. "Petrified beyond all hope!" She falls to the floor, dragging Brandon down beside her.

Tad flushes the evil spirit out of its corner, and it begins running toward us, growling and snarling now. It is low to the ground, and appears to be wearing a bandit's mask.

It's a raccoon, not a ghost. A very angry raccoon, by the looks of things.

Mrs. Keckley has fallen to her knees and tries to revive Mrs. Lincoln; Brandon and Mr. Goodchild form a protective wall in front of her; and the president shakes his head. "Well, I'll be," he says. "You were both right and wrong, Tad, a condition I've noticed is unique in no way. Noises you did hear; a ghost it was not."

The raccoon skids to a halt in front of us, snarls, and clatters back the way it came. Tad, not quite sure what to do now, jumps aside as the raccoon comes near.

"Sir?" says Mr. Hay. "Do you want me to get rid of it?"

"No, John, leave the critter be, at least for this night. He has done us no substantive harm, so far as I can make out. He has given Mother a spell, I'll grant him that. But I suspect she'll recover soon enough."

Tad comes running back over to his father, who picks him up and says, "So you see, Tad, when we know but half of the truth, our tendency is to fill the other half with all manner of blackest fear and worry. It sadly reminds me of myself, and what I do not know of General Meade and Gettysburg: I can only conjure the worst, try as I might not to. Now, Tad, speak plainly, if you will: have you a prior acquaintance with our friend Mr. Raccoon?"

"Well, Pa," Tad says. "I didn't know it was going to get up here!"

"I believe, sir," says Mr. Goodchild, "that the raccoon was . . . *introduced* about a month ago. To keep the goat company, if I recall. I thought it had been . . . removed."

"You and your animals, Tad," the president says. "It will be the end of Mother, if nothing else. Now then, what are we to do with her? Mrs. Keckley, do tell: Is she awake? Can she be moved?"

"She is not awake, sir," Mrs. Keckley says. "She is dead out. I think we must carry her down."

"Then carry her we will," says the president. "Mr. Hay, Mr. Goodchild—pray take the front end. Master Brandon and I shall take the back."

And this is how the First Lady is brought out of the attic, down the stairs, and into her bedroom—three men and one boy, each carrying a limb. She's put on her bed, and then the president turns to us.

"I would like a word with you three," he says. "Privately. Mr. Hay? Please escort our young friends to my office. I shall be there in a second. First, I must get Master Tad here to bed."

"This way, please," Mr. Hay says. "Follow me." We are herded down the stairs to the second floor, and while Mr. Lincoln takes Tad to his bedroom, Mr. Hay leads Bev, Brandon, and me into the president's large private office.

Then he shuts the door, and locks it.

# FIFTEEN

"WHY DID HE LOCK the door?" Bev asks.

"Because President Lincoln wants to talk with us?" I say.

"What about?" says Brandon.

"I don't know. I guess we'll find out."

"Are we allowed to sit down?" Brandon says.

"I don't think we should," Bev says. "I think we should stand till he comes."

So we stand around for a minute or two, which gives me a chance to check for messages. I don't have just one text from Mr. Hart—I have ten.

He starts calm, but ends in a near panic. First he wants to know where we are, what we're doing, when we're coming back.

Then he starts to worry, and tells us we don't know what we're up against.

The last question, though, is what gets to me: He says: *Why are you in the White House and what are you doing there?*

I'm staring at my phone, trying to figure how it's possible for Mr. Hart to know our *precise* location, when I get another incoming.

That old tri-chord melody.

*You must be CAREFUL! You are being watched!*

"Dude," Brandon says. "Who you texting? Mr. Hart?"

"Yes," I tell him, and then fire one off: *So how does everyone know where we are?*

I show Bev and Brandon the texts. "How come everyone knows we're at the White House?" asks Bev. "Can they do that?"

"Seems like it," I say.

"Hey," Bev says. "I just remembered something." She takes out her own phone, but before she can do anything the door is unlocked and in walk President Lincoln and Mr. Hay. We try to put away our phones but it's too late—they noticed.

But President Lincoln says not a word. Instead, he walks across the office and sits at his desk, and motions for Mr. Hay to arrange three chairs in front of it. We take our seats, and Mr. Hay at first stands behind the president.

Then Mr. Hay begins pacing around the office, very

much like a prosecutor before the jury. In his hand are a stack of papers. The jury—and the judge, from what it seems like—is President Lincoln. "Mr. President," Mr. Hay begins, "we have before us three children. No one knows who they are, where they came from, or can vouch for them in any way. They wear peculiar clothes and hold in their hands most peculiar devices. We do not know what they wish to accomplish or what they hope to achieve. But there does seem to be an inescapable conclusion, Mr. President. I submit to you that these children are not from here. I say: they are foreign operatives of some sort!"

When he is finished, my phone emits a little chirp. The chirp Bev, Brandon, and I have heard since the day we were born, and a million times since.

We pretend we don't hear a thing.

Then it chirps again.

President Lincoln drums his fingers on his desk. "I believe one of your devices is emitting a sound. Either that, or we have ghosts in this very room. Mr. Hay? Did you not hear something?"

"I did, sir. Twice. A most peculiar sound."

"Mr. Hay," President Lincoln says, "if you please." He nods his head in my direction, and then Mr. Hay walks over to me and snatches my phone from my fingers.

"Sir, I believe I have discovered the purpose of these objects. They are . . . miniature messaging machines. Right here, there are . . . words."

Mr. Hay brings my phone over to President Lincoln. He uses a letter opener to push it around a little, like he's trying to spring a trap. Or maybe it's the bomb thing that has him worried. "Mr. Hay, what led you to conjecture that this is a 'miniature messaging machine,' as you put it?" asks the president. "I do not see any message, Mr. Hay. It is blank."

"There were words, Mr. President. Lit up, as if there were candles somehow hidden inside. . . . I'm not sure how exactly to explain it. . . . This is a phenomenon with which I am unfamiliar. Perhaps we should have these more closely examined by our manufacturing experts in the War Department."

"Quite unnecessary, Mr. Hay. We have before us three persons who will most readily supply us with all the answers we seek. I must say, this device is most curious. Indeed, I would say it is quite astonishing, though none of you seem astonished in the least. Tell me—how did you acquire it? Where was it made? *How* was it made? Is one person responsible for its design and construction—or many?"

But before we can say anything, my phone chirps again. Incoming.

The screen lights up, and the president can see it for himself this time.

"What have we here?" says the president. He puts on his glasses, peers down at my phone, and begins reading aloud the latest text from Mr. Hart.

*Cannot say. BTW, we have reason to believe Kurtis no longer in DC.*

President Lincoln takes off his glasses and frowns. "*DC*, I assume, stands for 'District of Columbia.' Kurtis, I know not. But what mean the letters *BTW*?"

Before we can answer, another incoming from Mr. Hart. The president stares at it an extra second this time before reading it aloud. *Also possible iTime app not fully functional. Stand by for further instructions.*

"iTime?" President Lincoln says. "What is this?"

Should I tell him we're from the twenty-first century, we have the ability to travel back and forth in time, and we know how everything is *supposed* to turn out?

I really, really, really, *really* don't think so. What if he asks about his own future? Would I tell him he'll be assassinated in less than two years while attending a play at Ford's Theater?

No way. I don't want to lie; not to Honest Abe. But I can play dumb or change the subject. "Well, Mr. President," I begin, "I'm not really sure you want to know. Maybe it's better that you don't."

"Why would that be?"

"Because you aren't supposed to know. It could influence things."

"Young man, you are describing the nature of this office. It is my express obligation to influence things."

"I understand that, sir. You're supposed to influence the present, though. Not the future."

"The future?"

"Yes."

"Are you fortune-tellers, then? All matter of marvel this day. First we have a communicator with the deceased, and now we have fortune-tellers who can tell us of our future. Wonders they may be, but at present I am far too concerned with the fortunes of the living."

"He does not speak the truth, Mr. President," says Mr. Hay. "Fortune-telling is as fraudulent as anything Lord Colchester could dream up. I am beginning to have grave suspicions about these three. Where are they from? What business do they have? How is it they possess these . . . objects . . . which we have never seen the likes of before? I advise we proceed with the utmost caution. I think no part of their story will bear the slightest scrutiny."

"Let us not be hasty in our judgment, John," says the president. "We need only learn one thing at a time. I first desire to know how this object of yours operates. Pray show me."

I don't feel I can hold him off any longer, so I come around to his side of the desk. "Well, it's really pretty easy. First, tap this, right here. That gets you to what's called the home screen. Then swipe, like this," I say, demonstrating. "Where it says 'slide to unlock.'" He manages to get it open on the first try.

"Phone," he says, reading the icons. "Mail. Sports Center. iTunes Store. Camera? Is this capable of photography?" Before I can answer, he pokes the Camera icon.

It's set to FaceTime, so the first thing President Lincoln sees is President Lincoln.

"Egads!" he says. "Who in the world is this morbid creature!"

"Press here," I tell him, and he does, taking a selfie for all time.

Then the president shows Mr. Hay, Bev, and Brandon his selfie.

"Do not say it," he says. "I have seen myself. A most melancholy and gloomy man, I fear, by outward appearance. Is this what my generals see when they speak to me? The soldiers in the field? To say nothing of Mary and Tad. And what is called for now, at this, the decisive hour, is the very opposite of gloom and melancholy. Mr. Hay—do you not agree?"

"I wouldn't say gloomy, sir. Or melancholy. Concerned, perhaps?"

"John, I beg you, do not try to gloss up the mud patch. My countenance precedes me, on its own accord, whether I will it to or not. I should run myself if I saw such a face approach. What can be done? The Union may depend upon a gaggle of men, hitherto unknown to one another, defending a few yards of ground—every ounce will be required of them, every last drop of blood, and if in their minds they think of this"—he points to the picture—"they may not be able to summon that last spark of courage and energy that they so surely will require."

"Try another," Brandon says. "Think of something good. You know—happy thoughts."

"Happy thoughts?" says President Lincoln. "What an unusual conception."

"I think of horses," Brandon says. "It gets me psyched."

"Psyched?" says the president. "Did you say *psyched*? What is the meaning of this word?"

"It means getting yourself in the right frame of mind," Bev says. "Like before a big speech. You get yourself ready to hit one out of the park."

"Hit what out of the park?" the president says, but smiles. "No need to explain. Your intent is clear. Perhaps . . . we could take another?"

"Sure," I say, and get the phone ready. "Just tap here when you're ready."

"I shall think of our Founding Fathers. Washington, Jefferson, Franklin, Adams, Hamilton, the whole lot of them. How many years ago was it—eighty-odd—that they conceived of a new nation. This—not my sad face—is what I want our brave soldiers to be thinking about at the critical hour. The enduring existence of these United States."

"Four score and seven years ago, to be exact," says Brandon. "If you want to get kind of poetic about it."

The president's eyes light up. "Capital idea," he says, almost to himself. "I must remember that." Then he snaps a new picture.

It's a keeper. He looks noble, determined, even majestic—an amazing change in just a few seconds, but this time he knew he was taking his picture and got himself psyched.

"Better," he says, pleased. "Far better. I am not a vain man, for I have little to be vain about, but at least this one is not so grim. Perhaps it may be useful."

Then the president suddenly stands up. "Mr. Hay, please escort our guests safely out—perhaps you could take care of their arrangements for the night. Allow them to take their objects with them, for I wish to see them no more. I cannot allow myself to be burdened unduly with secondary matters. I must return to the telegraph office to see if there is news. This blindness vexes me so. How I wish I could be at that battlefield . . . how I wish I could know what is going on. If only there were a way!"

# SIXTEEN

**M**R. HAY WALKS US out of the president's office, but not out of the White House as well. Instead he finds Mr. Goodchild, the butler, on the ground floor, and hands us over to him.

"Do something with these children, Mr. Goodchild," Mr. Hay says. "I don't care what. But do not, I beg you, allow either the president or Mrs. Lincoln to encounter them again. They have both had far too much to deal with today."

"Are they free to leave, then, Mr. Hay?" Mr. Goodchild asks.

"I suspect they have nowhere to go, Mr. Goodchild. It is night, this is Washington City, and it will not do to have them wandering about. I trust you will come up with a suitable arrangement. By morning, however, they must be gone, Mr. Goodchild—understood?"

"Perfectly, sir," Mr. Goodchild says.

"Very well. I must join the president in the telegraph office." He gives us one last glance, shakes his head in dismay, turns on his heel, and exits the White House.

"Come with me," Mr. Goodchild says.

We hesitate, but not for long. What else are we going to do? So we follow Mr. Goodchild, semi-reluctantly, until he opens up the door to the basement and says, "This way."

"Down there?" says Brandon. "It's dark."

"You will have this," says Mr. Goodchild, handing over a lantern. It has one candle, maybe five inches high, which throws off a very dim light. "It will suffice."

"And what are we supposed to do down there?" asks Bev.

"There is a room," Mr. Goodchild says. "It has cots. It is used for when there are extra kitchen workers, but this night you may use it. I'm afraid there is no other choice."

He descends the staircase, his own lantern flickering. He leads us down to the lower level, through a storage room, and to a door at the end of a dingy and dirty hall. He swings the door open. "There you are," he says. "I shall wake you at dawn, and you shall leave very quietly and disturb no one."

The room is small, dark, cramped, and has a dirt floor. Three bare cots are against three of the four walls. No other furniture. Mr. Goodchild walks to a far corner, lights a gas lamp. The room looks even worse, if possible, with more light.

"Any questions?" asks Mr. Goodchild.

We have a few. Brandon wants to know about the facilities. I want to know about breakfast. Bev wants to know what's making that noise she hears—she says it sounds like something's crawling around on the floor.

Mr. Goodchild gives us the answers—a pot, nothing, and mice—and then bids us good night.

We stake out our cots, sit down. "This is good," I say. "Perfect, as a matter of fact."

"Mel," says Bev. "Don't be delusional. It's about as far from perfect as it gets. And I am not going to lie down on this thing," she adds. "Ever."

I take out my phone to reread Mr. Hart's texts. "Be careful. We are being watched. The iTime app maybe doesn't work. And Kurtis is no longer in DC, which means he could be anywhere. I'm not seeing many positive signs here, are you guys?"

"No," Bev says. "And don't forget, we're considered 'enemy combatants' now, right?"

"Right. According to Kurtis's letter. Delivered by that Pinkerton detective guy, who's probably still keeping an eye on us."

"Yeah, well, I've been thinking," Bev says. "It just occurred to me when we were in the president's office. Remember what Professor Moncrieff said?"

"About what?"

"Brandon asked him how his trackers were going to find Kurtis—it's a big country. The professor said he added new functionality, but he didn't explain it. What do you think he was talking about? Hold on," Bev says, and scrolls through her phone. "Found it!" she says. "I have a new icon: iTracker. I bet it's like GPS, only it works in time as well as location."

Bev taps it. Her screen says: UNAUTHORIZED USER. REQUEST DENIED.

"So this is how the trackers were going to find Kurtis," Bev says. "Impressive."

"I wonder if Kurtis has the same thing," I say. "To track us. Maybe that's how he knew we had arrived. And was able to send his goon Hubie around to give us his letter."

"Probably right," agrees Bev. "Though I'm not sure what we can do about it at this point. But let's try iTime," she says, and taps that. Nothing happens. She taps it again.

The iTime app starts to dissolve. Then it reconstructs itself, only to dissolve again. Finally a message appears, with the iTime icon now a crumbled heap: UNAUTHORIZED USER. REQUEST DENIED. ENJOY YOUR STAY.

"Well, isn't that just great," Bev says.

"Can I say something now?" says Brandon.

"What, Brandon?" says Bev.

"I think I know why we're in Washington and Kurtis isn't."

"Why's that, Brandon?"

"Because he *lured* us here. And now that we're here, we can't leave. But he can. And I think I know where he went."

"Where?"

"Gettysburg. That's his plan all along."

"Okay," Bev says, waving her hand. "Thank you, Brandon. It doesn't help at all, but thank you anyway."

My phone trills, and I see an incoming. *URGENT.*

"Urgent what?" Bev says, and then I get another incoming. *URGENT. STAND BY.*

"Our further instructions," I say, "are coming any minute."

It takes nearly three before they arrive. *Proceed to Gettysburg ASAP! Kurtis has just arrived! You must arrive no later than tomorrow, July 2. FIND KURTIS AT ALL COSTS!! HE WILL ATTEMPT TO CHANGE OUTCOME OF BATTLE!!!!!*

"See?" says Brandon. "Just like I told you—though you didn't believe me!"

We stare, dumbfounded, at my phone. "Okay then," I finally say. "Simple enough. Which way to Gettysburg?"

"It's the middle of the night, Mel," says Bev. "And we're in the basement of the White House. I'm not sure there's anything we can do right at the moment. Text him back—we'll have to come up with a plan."

"Even President Lincoln wants us to go to Gettysburg, though he couldn't say so," says Brandon. "Not out loud, he couldn't. Not in so many words. But he definitely was sending us a message."

"Yes," says Bev. "His message was, 'Somebody please get rid of these kids so I never have to see them again.'"

"Wrong!" says Brandon. "You weren't listening. And according to Mrs. Lincoln, I have special powers. So let me tell you what he *really* meant: he wants *us* to go to Gettysburg. To be his ears and eyes. He practically spelled it out for us in black and white. He just couldn't say so in front of that Mr. Hay dude."

"I heard no such thing, Brandon," Bev says.

"Me neither," I say.

"Then you weren't *listening*," says Brandon. "He said, 'How I wish I could be at that battlefield, and know what's going on . . . if only there were a way!' Get it? He's basically begging us to go there for him. It's like he's sending us on a mission—*telegraphically*."

Our first instinct—Bev and me, that is—is to dismiss this out of hand. But maybe, just maybe, it's not as weird as it sounds. "Well," I say, "I don't know about reading President Lincoln's mind, but Mr. Hart has the same idea. The problem is, there's no way to get to Gettysburg. No way to get there in time, that is."

"Yes, you can," says a voice from outside the door. "I know how."

# SEVENTEEN

**B**RANDON GETS UP, OPENS the door. It's Tad. In his pajamas.

"How long . . . where'd you come from?" I ask.

"I know *everything* that's going on!" Tad says. "I heard Pa slam the door to his office and I figured there was going to be some action . . . then I followed you all and Mr. Hay down the stairs and I saw him talk to Mr. Goodchild. So I sneaked down here when he left. What's this iTracker thing you're talking about?"

"It's none of your business, Tad," says Bev.

"Wait," says Brandon. "Did you say we *can* get to Gettysburg?"

"Of course you can—by tomorrow! It's easy! All you have to do is take the trains—and Willie and me have collected all the timetables! We got near every train time-table in the whole country. We keep 'em in a box underneath Willie's bed. Of course, Ma doesn't want me to go into Willie's room anymore . . . but maybe I could make an exception. On account of how important this is. Who's Kurtis?"

"Just a guy," I say. "What time tomorrow do you think we could get there?"

"Depends. On the schedules. I could go get 'em for you . . . if I were inclined. But maybe I'm not."

"Are you looking for a bribe?" Bev says. "Or what?"

"I wouldn't call it a bribe, exactly," says Tad. "More like a favor."

"Spell it out, Tad," I say. "We can't read your mind."

"All right. I want to see one of those things you have. And I want you to show me how it works. Mr. Hay said he thinks it's a mini-messaging machine, didn't he?"

"He must have been hanging around outside the door," Bev says. "Talk about spies, Tad. You got it beat."

"I ain't a spy!" Tad protests. "Just watching out for Pa! 'Cause you never know!"

We exchange glances. We know—unfortunately—the fate of President Lincoln, but of course Tad doesn't. And since our stated and sincere intention is make sure everything in history happens as it's *supposed* to happen, we can't tell Tad that in less than two years his father will be assassinated by John Wilkes Booth.

No matter how much we'd want to prevent it.

"Get the schedules first," I tell him. "Then we'll see about showing you . . . the thing."

"So we got a deal?" Tad says.

"We'll think about it," I say.

"You better hurry," Brandon says. "Before we change our mind. We can find our own way to the train station, Tad. It can't be that hard."

"I'll go get 'em and bring 'em right back!" Tad says, and is about ready to run out when Bev grabs him by the arm. "Listen," she says. "There's one other thing. You go to Mrs. Keckley's room and get my clothes. Because there is absolutely no way I am going to wear this ridiculous dress any longer. Got it, Tad?"

Tad nods his head, and ten minutes later he returns, carrying what looks to be an old cigar box filled to the brim with train schedules, and Bev's clothes.

"Now you guys wait," Bev says. "I'll be right back."

We're not sure where she goes, but in a few minutes she returns dressed the way she was before, and throws the dress on the cot. "Okay, Tad," Bev says. "What have you got?"

Tad puts the box on Brandon's cot, which is closest to the lantern, and we all lean in to take a closer look. Tad begins taking out the schedules one by one. The Baltimore and Ohio. Illinois Central Railroad. The Camden and Amboy. The Erie Railroad. The Pennsylvania Railroad. Toledo, Wabash, and Western Railroad Company.

"We near memorized 'em!" Tad says. "Willie and me,

we spent hours lookin' at these and we came up with all sorts of ways to get from one place to the other! Why, I can tell you practically without looking what you'll have to do to get to Gettysburg!"

There's no stopping Tad when he gets wound up. "First of all, it ain't more than eighty or ninety miles to Gettysburg, though you can't take just one train all the way. It's simple. From Washington City you go to Baltimore, from Baltimore you switch onto the Northern Central at the Bolton Station, and then you ride that up to Hanover Junction, in Pennsylvania, and then you go on over to Gettysburg on the Hanover Line. If you leave tomorrow morning and take the first train to Baltimore, you should be in Gettysburg no later than the afternoon. Easy as pie! Excepting for one thing—you're going to need money to pay for your tickets. You have any?"

"That part of it we can handle," I say, remembering the gold coins I stuffed in my pocket. I knew they would come in handy. "When's the first train to Baltimore, Tad?"

"Why, eight o'clock in the morning, same as it is every day! Everyone knows that!"

"If we could just write down the times . . . and the stations . . . then I think we'll be good," I say.

Tad grabs all the schedules and shoves them back into his box. "We had a deal," he says. "Remember?"

"We did," I say.

"And a deal's a deal," says Tad. "So let me see one of those things."

"You mean this?" Brandon says, and waves his phone

in front of Tad, who tries to snatch it. "Not so fast, bud," says Brandon. "Not so fast. This is something we only let *friends* see. You get me, Tad? Friends."

"But I'm a friend," Tad says hopefully.

"What about those?" Brandon says, pointing to the timetables he has clutched in his hands. "We haven't copied them down yet. The trains to Gettysburg."

"And we need a way out of here, Tad," I chip in. "A secret way, where no one spots us. Doesn't the White House have tunnels or something?"

"Would I get to . . . play with it?" Tad asks, still hopeful.

"First things first, Tad. Fork over the timetables. Then you get to play."

His mind is already made up. He hands me the timetables.

"Hey, Tad," Brandon says. "Here's something pretty cool. You ever see this game called Clash of Clans?" And Brandon hands Tad his phone.

That pretty much is all we need. Clash of Clans will do the rest, and there is no nine-year-old boy anywhere who has the power to resist.

Clash of Clans, in case you're unaware, is a free phone app, and in my humble opinion, totally dumb.

But I know maybe forty kids who've gone completely off the deep end with Clash of Clans. They talk about it *all* the time. Brandon and some of his dopey pals play it all the time, even in class, if they think they can get away with it.

They're *obsessed* with it, you could say. And up to two

minutes ago I would have said being obsessed with a game app was totally one hundred percent big-time *lame*.

Now?

Not so much.

Tad doesn't really ask a lot of questions once Brandon shows him how it works. Unlike Dr. Franklin, who insisted on learning as much as possible about the technology of an iPhone, Tad just wants to play.

I go through the timetables, and it takes me about fifteen minutes to figure everything out. Seeing how there is no paper or pens in our basement dungeon, I put all the info into my phone: Washington to Baltimore, Baltimore to Hanover Station, Hanover Station to Gettysburg. Should be a piece of cake, right?

I text Mr. Hart to let him know the plan. A minute later he texts back: *Acceptable. Check in when on train for further instructions.*

I turn off my phone to save power; our next problem will be prying Brandon's phone from Tad's greedy little fingers.

"Time's up, Tad," Brandon says. "Give it back."

"I ain't," Tad says. "I need to go up a level."

"Boys," Bev says, shaking her head, rolling her eyes. "What *is* it with you guys and computer games?"

"It's an app, Bev," says Brandon. "Not a computer game. There's a difference."

"No, there isn't," says Bev. "It's a stupid thing where you waste a colossal amount of time."

"Time's up, Tad," I say, putting the schedules back in the box. "Show us how to get out of here without being seen. There's a secret passageway, right? Somewhere?"

"Not that I know of," Tad says, gripping Brandon's phone even tighter.

"I'm pretty sure there is," I say.

"How would you know?" Tad says.

I almost slip, and tell him I saw it in a movie, or on a TV show—I don't really remember how I know. Or even if there is such a thing as a secret White House tunnel.

But I do know this: until we pry Clash of Clans from Tad, we'll never get out of the White House.

But this is when Bev proves herself to be especially useful—her favorite word.

She's super impatient, remember. Everybody knows it. Nine times out of ten, she won't even let you finish your sentence before cutting in and saying, "Okay, okay, what's your point?"

So, like, right now, Brandon and me are *wondering* how to pry Clash of Clans from Tad's hands.

*Contemplating* it.

Trying to figure out the *logistics*.

Bev? She doesn't bother *thinking* about it.

She just grabs Brandon's phone with one hand and uses her other hand to hold Tad off.

"Hey!" Tad squawks. "I ain't done!"

"You find us a way out," Bev says. "And then—if we feel like it—we might let you play some more."

"You can walk out the front door," Tad says. "Same way you came in."

"We told you. That's not happening. We need a secret way out, Tad, get it? Now, you want to play some more or what?" Bev dangles Brandon's phone inches from Tad's eyes.

He tries to resist, he really does. But when's the next time he's going to get a chance to play Clash of Clans? Never, that's when.

"Well," Tad says. "There might be a way. I can't promise anything, though. How long would I get to have it?"

"You can't *have* it," says Brandon. "You can *use* it. That's all."

"How long?" persists Tad.

"Thirty minutes," Brandon says. "No more, no less."

"If I told you about a secret tunnel," Tad says, "then it wouldn't be secret, would it?"

"That's a fair point, Tad," I say. "We'd have to swear an oath, wouldn't we?"

"That's right," Tad says. "You got to swear on your life. 'Cause no one can ever know."

"Fine with me," says Brandon.

"Me too," I say.

"Whatever," says Bev, but we're already on our way.

# EIGHTEEN

TAD LEADS US OUT of our room, across one narrow hallway, down another. Our candles provide the only light. Finally we come to a back wall, and it seems as if we can go no farther. But then Tad moves some empty crates, revealing a very small door, maybe three feet high. It has a padlock on it.

"Now you need to swear," Tad says, "that you will never, never, never tell no man, woman, child, or dog that there exists a secret White House tunnel. You ready?"

We solemnly nod our heads and mumble that we'll never tell.

Then Brandon, Tad, and me spit in our hands. We wait for Bev, who scrunches up her face in total disgust and then does the deed herself.

Then we shake hands all around. Our deal is sealed.

"Now give me the game," Tad says. "I really need to get to the next level."

I flip the lock. "What are we supposed to do now, Tad? Stand here and cast a spell?"

"That's extra," Tad says. "I took you this far."

The candlelight is getting eerie. And I hear strange noises. Things moving about, I think. Not raccoons again. Mice, maybe. And boy, I'm sure glad I don't believe in ghosts.

I don't, right?

"Extra what?" says Brandon.

"Extra time."

"For what—unlocking this? Do you even have a key?"

"I might. Another thirty minutes?"

"Open it," says Bev. "You didn't say anything about a lock and key."

"Shhh," says Tad. "You don't want everyone to know what we're up to, do ya?"

"Listen, you little . . ."

"Bev, easy," I say. "Tad, where does this lead to?"

"Department of the Treasury. Across the street."

"Directly into the Department of the Treasury, or just outside it?" I ask.

"Inside. From there you'll have to make your way out on your own, 'cause I ain't going with you." He reaches into his pocket and pulls out a key. "Me and Willie found this extra one. Lying around, you could say. It'll be handy, if the Rebs ever do come."

"How's it going to help us if the door on the other side is locked?" says Bev.

"It ain't," says Tad. "Never is. What kind of escape route do you think this is? Folks would just get trapped in the tunnel and that would be the end of 'em."

"You sure?"

"Sure I'm sure! Me and Willie tested it out once. Door swings right open."

"And when was this?"

"I don't know, maybe a couple of years ago."

"And nothing's changed since then?"

"Of course not! It's the president's secret escape plan! Who would change things?"

"I can think of a few candidates," Bev says. "But all right. I guess we'll find out when we get to the other side."

"We'll need the lantern," I say. "And some extra candles."

"Fine," says Tad, and hands me the lantern. "You can find all the candles you need in the kitchen."

"And he has to prove the key works," says Bev. "Before any deal."

Tad agrees, inserts the key into the lock, and it pops open. "See?" he says. Then he locks it, and holds out his hand. "Two hours," he says. "And not a minute less."

"Deal," I say. And then for two hours we sit there,

on the cold basement floor, while Tad plays Clash of Clans. We take turns falling asleep and keeping guard—on Tad, who nobody trusts not to run off with Brandon's phone. I do a little exploring and grab about a dozen candles from the kitchen. Finally time is up. He asks for five minutes, but a deal is a deal. He hands over the phone, unlocks the padlock, and into the tunnel we go.

Our inventory of assets: three phones, a handful of gold coins, a lantern, and extra kitchen candles.

"Well, good luck," Tad says. "You can come back, you know. Any time you want."

"We just might, Tad," I say. "You never can tell."

"All you need do is follow the train schedules. They ain't never wrong." Then we hear him close the door behind us, and lock us in. Or out, depending on how you look at it.

"Okay, guys," I say. "All we have to do is cross the tunnel, and we're home free. Ready?"

One little lantern.

One long tunnel.

We can't stand up, of course. We have to crouch down, or else our heads will scrape the ceiling. Things would have to get real bad if President Lincoln were forced to escape this way, and even then I'm not sure if he could crouch down low enough.

"I'm not liking this," says Brandon. "It's leaking some-place. What if it caves in?"

"It won't," I say, although I was thinking the same thing.

"So why's it wet? And what are those noises?"

We listen. We definitely have company in here. I'm not sure if they're rats, mice, raccoons, or goblins, but something is scurrying around just past where our light reaches.

Bev turns on her flashlight app. It lights up the tunnel, all right, but doesn't provide us any more comfort.

"That app will use up your power, Bev," I say.

"I know," she says, turning it off. "Just wanted to see what we're getting into. I'll go first, all right? Give me the lantern."

She takes the lantern and starts off.

I'm okay with Bev leading the way. But I'm just a few steps behind her when I realize that no one's behind *me*.

"Brandon! Where are you?"

I see darkness behind me. Ahead, Bev keeps plowing through, taking the lantern—and the light—with her.

"I can't do it," Brandon says from twenty yards away. "I'm claustrophobic."

"Since when?"

"Since now. I never knew."

"Oh for crying out loud," I say. "Bev! Wait! We have a problem down here."

Bev is Bev, remember. I'm pretty sure—I'm absolutely positive, in fact—that's she not going to be too thrilled with any delays or slowdowns.

"What problem, Mel?"

"Brandon. Apparently all of a sudden he's claustrophobic."

"Good for him. Is he going to come along or not?"

"I think not."

"Are you serious?"

"I think so."

"Oh brother," Bev says, in full peeve mode. "You two are nothing but deadweight sometimes, you know?"

But the lantern starts coming back down the tunnel. She gets to me and keeps going, and then both of us walk all the way back to the starting line, where Brandon is sitting down on what looks to be the legless top half of a chair.

We can tell at once that poor Brandon is spooked. Bev loses her peeve and gets right to it.

"We're not staying here, Brandon," she says. "We can't. You know that, right?"

"I know it in my mind," Brandon says.

"Well, that's good enough. I've already been halfway through. Nothing to it. I tell you what. You hold the lantern and go first. We'll be right behind you. We'll be out of here in no time."

"It's dark," Brandon says. "And creepy. Seen any snakes? I hate snakes. I got bit once by a snake. I was six. They had to take me to the emergency room."

"No snakes," Bev says. She's grabbed Brandon's hand, and folded his fingers around the lantern handle. "Just one little step. That's all."

"Really?"

"Yep. And then another one. Before you know it, we'll be on the other side. Trust me, Brandon. Just one little step."

He's sweating, the lantern is shaking in his hand, and even I can feel the lump in his throat. But he moves his right foot a few inches forward.

Then his left foot. His right again. He begins to make progress. Bev is holding on to his belt, and I'm right behind her.

We couldn't go any slower, but in fifteen minutes we're maybe halfway across.

We're not bitten by snakes or rats, and we don't come across any goblins or ghouls. Our little trek is surprisingly straightforward and uneventful.

Which is why I'm worried when we come to the door at the end of the tunnel. The one Tad said is never locked?

It's locked.

"Well, isn't this just wonderful," says Bev. "Who could have *possibly* anticipated this?"

But that's not all.

Because not only is the door locked, but we also hear *voices*.

On the other side of the door.

We don't know if they're people or ghosts, but right now all of us—and not just Brandon—are, like, *totally* spooked.

Then it gets worse.

We hear a click.

Then a clack.

Then a clank. The kind of clank you might hear if someone just unlocked a lock and tossed it to the ground.

We step back, the lantern and our phones our only weapons.

The door handle is jiggled. Then it starts to slowly swing open. . . .

CHOO-CHOO CHARLIES

# NINETEEN

PRESIDENT LINCOLN WAS RIGHT.

Whether it's sounds in an attic, or a swinging door at the end of a tunnel, you fear most what you *imagine*—not what is in front of your face.

I *imagined* that behind the swinging door was Hubie, or Kurtis himself, or maybe Frankenstein and Godzilla and the Green Goblin all rolled into one.

But no.

It is only Mr. Goodchild, the White House butler, and Mrs. Keckley, the dressmaker. They're holding candles, blankets, and food.

"You scared us!" I say.

"We know, we know," says Mr. Goodchild. "There was no other way. This end is locked, despite what Tad might have told you. Otherwise there would be no protecting the other end."

"How . . . how did you know?" Bev asks.

"Discretion," says Mrs. Keckley, "has never been one of Tad's virtues. When he came to get your things, he was in such a great rush . . . I rather had my suspicions. And then Mr. Goodchild overheard the . . . the discussions about the trains."

"I have the feeling everyone overhears everything at the White House," Brandon says. "Is there any way to keep a secret?"

"There is not," says Mrs. Keckley. "In this case, all to the good. Whatever your plans are, you will not be permitted to leave Washington City without one of these." She waves three pieces of paper in front of us. "They are passes, dear children. In case you have forgotten, we are in a war. No one is supposed to come or go without a duly authorized travel pass. You may thank Mr. Hay for providing these."

She hands us each a travel pass. "Now, there is no place for you to go until dawn. We brought you blankets and something to eat before you leave. Mr. Goodchild and I will take turns staying with you. But in the morning you must be gone, and never a word about this to anyone. Understood?"

It seems like the best deal we're likely to get. We spread out our blankets and make ourselves as comfortable as we can. Mrs. Keckley pulls up an old crate and sits down.

I conk out in about thirteen seconds. There's something comforting about lying at Mrs. Keckley's feet.

It seems like only thirteen seconds later, though, I'm awakened.

"Mel! Let's go!"

It's Brandon.

It takes me a second to realize I'm not in my nice warm bed at the Fredericksville School—I'm on the ground outside a tunnel in the basement of the Treasury Building.

In Washington City.

And instead of Mrs. Keckley seated on her old crate, Mr. Goodchild is hovering over us.

"We have to go, Mel," Brandon says. "The train leaves at eight, right?"

"Right," I say, sitting up. "What time is it?"

"Twenty to," says Brandon. "We better hurry, or else we'll miss it."

We thank Mr. Goodchild, who is eager for us to leave so he can go back to the normal craziness of the White House. Then we run upstairs and find a taxi to take us to the Baltimore and Ohio train station on New Jersey Avenue.

We're not talking a Yellow Cab taxi either. With a meter and all that. Nope, this is a horse-and-buggy type of deal. The driver who takes us by carriage smells like sour milk. When he lets us out at the station, which is just up from the Capitol, he practically keels over when

I give him a whole gold coin and tell him to keep the change.

"Wait a minute," Brandon says now. We're standing on New Jersey Avenue, waiting to go inside the station to catch the eight o'clock train to Baltimore, and Brandon is staring down the road. "What's up with the Capitol? Something's missing."

Sure enough, something *does* seem to be missing. The dome is done, everything is gleaming white, the whole thing is huge . . . but something isn't right.

"Isn't there supposed to be a statue or something on top?" says Bev.

She's right. The dome's shortchanged. "They'll stick it on later," I say.

"They should pave some of these dirt roads before they do anything else," Brandon says. "If you ask me."

"We'll tell the president your suggestion, Brandon," I say, "the next time we see him. Now, are we ready?" I check my phone for the notes I took based on Willie Lincoln's timetables.

Bev and Brandon nod their heads, and into the station we go.

Crowds of people are heading into and out of the train station, and as soon as we walk in I feel a thousand sets of eyes upon us. It's a hot morning in July, but every man has on at least pants, a long-sleeved shirt, and a hat; every woman wears an elaborate dress and an even fancier hat. We're the only ones who seem completely put out by the heat, which is ten times inside the station what it was on the outside. I'm not sure when air conditioning was invented, but it sure wasn't in 1863.

I see about two hundred men with walrus-style mustaches of the kind worn by that guy Hubie, and I'm keeping in mind what Kurtis wrote in his note: that we will be considered enemy combatants, suitable targets for termination of the most prejudicial variety. That could be a knife in the back at pretty much any time, I'm guessing. Not that it's going to stop us, but still. It would be nice to take a trip someplace without a major dose of the creeps.

"How do we get tickets?" says Brandon.

"How about we try the ticket window," Bev says. "You've been on a train before, right, Brandon?"

"I can't say I have."

Bev rolls her eyes, then leads us straight to the ticket window and asks for three tickets to Baltimore. We're asked to show our travel passes, which we have, thanks to Mrs. Keckley and Mr. Hay.

I pay for the tickets with one of my coins. "What's this?" says the ticket agent.

"A gold coin."

"I can see that. You need greenbacks. That's paper money."

"Well, can't you take it instead?"

"I'm not supposed to. Besides, I can't give you change except in greenbacks."

"We'll take whatever change you give us."

The man shrugs, takes the coin, and hands over three tickets and seven large ten-dollar bills. One side is green—hence the word *greenback*—and the other side has a picture of President Lincoln. I stuff the bills into the pocket where I keep the other coins and grab the tickets, and we find our track. Then we take our seats in the third car of a seven-coach train. It's so crowded we're lucky to sit together. I'm in first and take the seat next to the window.

A guy in front of us turns around and glares at us. He has a thick red mustache, which maybe he thinks will make up for his thin red hair but doesn't. "Where's your parents?" the guy says, as if it's any of his business.

"My mom's in an ashram," Brandon says. "In Taos, New Mexico."

"What's an ashram?" the guy says, as if he's certain he's not going to like the answer.

"It's a place where you go to become one with the universe," Brandon says.

"One with what?"

"One with the universe."

"What's that supposed to mean?" By now another person has turned around and faces us. A lady. Who's wearing an enormous hat and a billowy flowered dress.

"Whoever are these children, Walter?" she says to the man, who is presumably her husband.

Walter narrows his eyes. "I'm not sure who they are, Dolores. Though I'm quite sure they have no business being on this train unaccompanied. Do you have paid tickets? Or did you sneak aboard? There have been numerous incidents of thievery and pickpockets on this line—numerous! I shall have a word with the conductor the minute I see him."

"Dude, we're not here to steal," Brandon says. "We got all the gold we need. Show him, Mel."

I jangle the gold coins in my pocket. "We're good," I say. "More than good."

"Hrmph," says Walter.

Dolores says, "What did the boy call you? *Dude?* Whatever does that mean?"

"It means they have no respect, and should be escorted off this train immediately. I swear I will have a word, Dolores. Just as soon as the conductor comes by."

They both *hrmph* this time and turn around in their seats. Other passengers have noticed, and we feel a distinct chill in the hundred-degree coach.

"Let's try to keep a low profile," Bev says.

"Good idea," I say. "And I don't know about you guys, but I'm starting to think this trip might not be as easy as it seemed. Notice all the soldiers?"

About a quarter of the train seems to be filled with soldiers—Union soldiers, of course—and more are coming on board. I look out the window and see one soldier being carried along on a stretcher, another walking with crutches, and another with only one arm. The soldiers are either going home or going to battle, but either way nobody seems too pleased. I think our best bet is to leave them alone.

The train's whistle blows. One long, one short. We're about to get moving.

Which is fine with me, because I want to get out of here. Washington City doesn't impress—it's hot, dirty, crowded, and nearly everyone has an attitude. Maybe that's what happens when you're in the middle of a civil war.

"All aboard!" we hear from behind us. The train lurches and chugs, gears grind, the engine coughs, wheels screech, and then we move. Six inches, a foot, tops. Then more lurching, grinding, coughing, screeching, and we move maybe another two feet.

At this rate, I'm beginning to doubt we'll ever get to Gettysburg in time to make a difference.

# TWENTY

A HALF HOUR LATER, WE'RE rolling along at a pretty good clip. My eyes get a little droopy, and my head starts to sag. Then I seem to be talking to my good old roommate, Benji. Benji and I have the same first class at 8:10 every morning. Algebra, with Mrs. Alford. She's so nice, Mrs. Alford. I don't understand everything all of the time, but at least she doesn't make me feel *bad* about it, like some other teachers I know. . . .

"Mel! Wake up!"

"It's cool, Benji," I say. "I'll get up in five minutes."

"Benji? Who's Benji?"

I open my eyes. It's Brandon poking me in the ribs, not Benji. And we're in a train, not in school.

"Aren't you supposed to let Mr. Hart know where we are?"

"Oh yeah," I say. "Thanks."

"Maybe I should take over text duty," says Bev. "At least I'm reliable."

"So am I," I say, getting up. "I'm going to walk around." In the last car I find some empty seats. I slide in, keeping my head low, take out my phone, and power up.

*On train,* I text. *First leg—DC to Baltimore.*

A minute later Mr. Hart texts back: *Good. Expected arrival Gettysburg?*

*Two p.m. If all goes according to plan.*

*Are you being followed?*

*No. Don't think so.*

*Are you positive?*

*No, but don't think so.*

*Beware strangers. Don't tell anyone where you're going. TRUST NO ONE!!!*

*Okay, take it easy. All good so far.*

*Check in next leg.*

*Roger that,* I say, and power down. Trust no one, beware of strangers—Mr. Hart sounds like our mother sometimes more than our teacher.

I put my phone away, lift my head, and in front of me, staring over the back of the seat ahead, are three boys.

Older boys.

Teenagers. Fifteen, maybe even sixteen.

"What's that there?" says the one in the middle. He has pimples on his chin and mean beady eyes. Thief's eyes, I'd say, not that I've ever personally come across an out-and-out thief before. But sometimes, somehow, you just know things right from the start.

The other two are no better. The one on the left has freckles. The one on the right has a big nose.

"Nothing," I say.

"Nothing? I'd say it's something. You put it in your pocket."

"And what're you doing back here anyway?" says Big Nose. "You get permission? Either of you guys give permission?"

"I did not," says Freckles. "Nor would I, not especially to some half-sized boy who don't even belong on this train. You lost your mama?"

"Careful," says Pimples. "He might cry. Now, you tell us what that thing is in your pocket, and maybe we'll let you go. Otherwise . . . what should we do?"

Big Nose scratches his head. "Well, I do not rightly know. We could throw him from the train, couldn't we?"

"We could indeed," says Pimples. "It would hurt, though, wouldn't it? Being throwed from a train?"

"Depends," says Freckles. "On if he lands on his head or lands on his backside."

"Now lookit here," says Pimples, narrowing his beady eyes even further, which I didn't think was possible. "This is our territory, we staked it out, and ain't no one allowed on our car. So now you got to pay the fine, fair and square. Show us what you put in your pocket, and if we like it, we'll keep it. If we don't like it, you owe us."

"Sounds fair to me," says Big Nose. "More than fair. And if he can't do neither, why, we'll just have to throw him from the train."

I've decided that the last thing I'll do is show these guys my phone. Unlike Tad Lincoln, they're all bigger than me, and tougher—I have no doubt that once they have my phone I'll never get it back.

Money, on the other hand, sounds reasonable, considering the situation. "Will you take gold?" I ask, though I know full well they'll never be satisfied with a single coin when they can have them all—unless, of course, the situation is changed.

"Gold?" says Pimples. "Sure, we'll take gold. Hand it over."

"I'll get it for you." I slide out, stand up; Freckles moves aside to let me by.

"Wait," says Pimples. "You get your gold and bring it back here. You have exactly one minute. If you don't come back, we're coming to get you—and we won't be in a good mood. You understand? One minute."

I nod my head, like I'm in full and complete agreement, and then take off up the aisle. Of course I won't return, and if they enter our car to try to get either my gold or my phone, I'll have reinforcements. As I approach the car door I'm feeling rather proud of myself, until I see, seated alone and pretending to a read a newspaper, that guy Hubie.

The Pinkerton detective dude, with the enormous walrus mustache. Currently employed by T.G.W., Inc.

The guy who gave us a letter that said, in part, that if he happened to see us again we would be—if I have the quote right—"eminently suitable targets for termination of the most prejudicial variety."

A phrase like that sticks in your mind.

I'm not sure what I should do here, exactly, or say. Hubie takes charge of the situation. He nods at me, tips his hat, and smiles.

# TWENTY-ONE

"U H, BRANDON?" I SAY. "BEV?"

"What?" says Bev.

"I think we got a problem. On board."

"You mean because it's hot, there's no air conditioning, and everyone's looking at us funny?"

"That plus something else. Remember Hubie? Who gave us the note from Kurtis?"

"Mel? Why is everything you say a question?"

"Everything I say is a question?"

"Are you trying to be wise guy?"

"Why would I try to be a wise guy? I'm trying to tell you guys we have problem, and its name is Hubie!"

"Hubie? Isn't that the dude with the giant mustache?" Brandon says.

"That's the dude," I say. "He has a giant mustache and

**142**

he gave us the note from Kurtis. And he said if he ever sees us again it won't be so friendly. Well, guess what?"

"Mel, what's your point? It might be helpful if you could just spit it out," says Bev.

I'm about to tell them when Walter, the guy ahead of us, turns around, glares, and says, "Hrmph." I lean in and keep my voice down.

"He's on this train," I say. "He's in the last passenger car."

"Get out of here!" says Brandon.

"No way!" says Bev. And then she punches me in the arm. Hard.

"Way," I say.

"But how could he know we're here?" says Brandon. "Weren't we supposed to lose him by taking the tunnel out of the White House?"

"That's what I thought. I guess the Pinkerton Agency has a lot of resources. Maybe he staked us out at the railroad station. Who knows how."

I can tell Bev and Brandon are as unhappy about it as I am. "I'm not cool," Brandon says, "with being considered an *enemy combatant*. I don't know how you guys feel about it."

"Obviously we're not *cool* with it either, Brandon," Bev says. "The question is, what do we do if he shows up in our car?"

"We won't have to do anything," Brandon says. "We'll be sitting ducks. Where we gonna go?"

This time Dolores—the lady from the seat ahead of

us—turns around to glare at us. "You are disturbing my tranquility," she says. "It is my firm belief that children should be seen and not heard."

"Lady," Brandon mutters under his breath, "you are really starting to get on my nerves."

Bev pokes him in the ribs. "Shush, Brandon," she says. "I don't think kids in this time talk like that to adults. She might have a heart attack if she hears you."

"So that's a good thing, right?"

"Wrong, Brandon. Then they might have to stop the train. And where would that leave us?"

"Maybe in a better place, Bev. Right now we're stuck in a train with some crazy dude with a giant mustache out to get us."

Finally our train starts to gather speed—relatively speaking, that is—and as it does, it gets louder and louder inside, so we have to speak louder and louder to hear each other. I look out the window. Even though it *sounds* like we're going fast, and the wheels on the rails are creaking and squeaking with the effort, nothing *outside* is zipping by or anything. And I know zipping—I've taken the Amtrak Acela train a couple of times with my dad, and that thing *zips*.

"You think it makes sense?" I say. "For all of us to be sitting together? Maybe we should split up. It would increase our chances of—"

I'm just about to say the word "surviving" when the passenger car door behind us slides open. It's not Hubie, though; it's my three new best friends, Freckles, Big Nose, and Pimples. I haven't even had a chance to warn Bev and Brandon, I was so busy talking about Hubie.

Pimples leads the way. I haven't seen any of them standing up till now, and I'm surprised: they're each shorter than I expected.

"Lookie here," says Pimples. "He has friends. A boy and a girl. How nice. Mind if we sit?"

"There's no room, obviously," snaps Bev. "Find someplace else."

"Whoa," says Pimples. "That's none too friendly. Hear that, boys? This girl here told us to be on our way." He looks at me. "This your sister?"

"I'm not his sister," Bev says. "Not that it's any of your business. Now, we told you, there's no room. Feel free to get out of here."

"I wasn't talking to you," says Pimples. "I was talking to *him*." He jabs me in the chest with his finger. "And now that's going to cost you double. On account of your friend here being so downright rude. Now fork it over. Like you promised."

"You know these guys, Mel?" asks Brandon.

"Just met. A few minutes ago. In the last car."

"That's right," says Big Nose. "And he promised us something, which we've come to get. 'Cause he said he'd bring it back to us, but he didn't. So he's a liar besides."

"What's this all about, Mel?" Bev says. "What did you promise them?"

"Gold," says Pimples. "That, or else he was going to give us that black thing he stuck in his pocket, all secret like. We saw him poking around on it. But then he stuck it in his pocket and wouldn't show us."

"And," says Freckles, "he was infringing on our territory. We staked it out, fair and square. Anyone goes into our territory has got to pay, one way or another."

Pimples puts his hand out. It hovers, at eye level, between me and Bev. "Gold," he says. "Two pieces. If you hold us up any longer, the price goes to three."

The nasty couple ahead of us—Walter and the Mrs.—provide no help. So just when things seem on the verge of getting physical—either one of the boys is going to grab me, or Bev is going to slap Pimple's hand away—we get assistance from the unlikeliest source: Hubie, the Pinkerton detective.

"Boys, boys, boys," Hubie says, putting his arms around the three of them. He then squeezes, bringing them closer together. "Do we have a problem here? Or is this just a friendly visit?"

Somehow Hubie's jacket is open, so all of us can see the rather large pistol he has in a holster strapped across his chest.

"No, sir," mumbles Pimples. "No problem, no problem at all. Just saying howdy to some fellow passengers."

"That's what I thought," Hubie says. "Now you run along, and don't let me catch you up here again. You hear?"

He then squeezes their shoulders again, and Freckles and Pimples wince. They each glare at us, and as they leave I hear one of them mutter, "We ain't done yet with you, not by a long shot."

When they're gone, Hubie looks at me. "Slide over," he says. "I'm going to sit for a spell."

It's no sense arguing with a grown man who probably weighs two hundred and fifty pounds, or more. I slide over.

It takes him a minute or so to lower himself down, settle in. "Phew," he says at last. "Hot, ain't it?"

We say nothing. This is the same man, after all, who said if he ever saw us again he wouldn't be so friendly. And who gave us a note from Kurtis.

And he's still carrying the leather satchel with the letters T.G.W., INC. stenciled on the side.

"Now, where you heading?" he asks.

"Baltimore," I say, before Bev and Brandon can answer.

"Baltimore?"

"Right."

"Got family in Baltimore?"

"Friends," I say.

"Friends," he repeats, as if he doesn't believe a word.

"Yep. Figure we'll hang out in Baltimore for a couple of days. Maybe a week or two. Keep out of everyone's way."

"Uh-huh," Hubie says. "Though I seem to remember you were told something else. Am I right?"

"Let me get this straight," Bev interrupts. "You're a Pinkerton detective?"

"I am indeed, young lady. And proud of it."

"So you were hired by someone—to provide services?"

"That's how it works."

"And if the person hiring you turns out to be a criminal himself—then what?"

"Then it's not for you to worry your pretty little head about, young missy."

"If someone tells me not to worry my pretty little head about it one more time," Bev says, "I will blow a cork, I swear."

"Don't want to see that," Hubie says. "But I did deliver a note to you all, and I am keeping an eye on you as well, in case you didn't take heed, which you didn't. And just so you know—I don't work alone. We had the entire White House covered from the time you went inside. Including the Department of the Treasury. You can't slip by the Pinkerton Agency so easy. But I'll be truthful with you. I'm not exactly sure what I'm supposed to do with you now, other than keep an eye on you. Having trouble reaching the . . . uh . . . the client. But I was told not to lose sight of you, so that's what I'm going to do. Until I hear otherwise."

With that, he folds his hands across his very ample chest, lowers his hat, and shuts his eyes.

# TWENTY-TWO

FIFTEEN MINUTES LATER THE train's whistle blows—a long, loud blast that nearly wakes Hubie up. But he merely snorts, as if a mosquito had landed on his nose, then returns to his slumber.

"Can he hear us?" Brandon asks.

"I don't know," I say.

Brandon leans over and whispers in my ear. "I don't think he knows where we're really headed."

I nod in agreement. Bev leans over and says, "What are you two whispering about?"

Brandon jerks his thumb at the sleeping Hubie. "What are we going to do with him?" he says.

"We need to lose him somehow," I say. "And I think maybe I have an idea."

I stand up, maneuver my way around Hubie just as

the conductor comes down the aisle. "Baltimore next and final stop!" he yells. "Ladies and gentlemen, Camden Station, Baltimore, next stop!"

Hubie wakes up with a grunt, sees me in the aisle, grabs me by the arm. "And where do you think you're going, young mister?"

"Facilities," I say. "Before the next stop."

I've got to find my bad boys before it's too late. I hustle through the cars until I come to theirs, and they are as nasty looking and defiant as ever, only this time it seems as if their mothers have corralled them. Three adult women, in any case. Everyone has stood up and is making preparations to get off the train. I fight my way through the crowded aisle until I am standing right behind Freckles.

"I came to bring your payment," I say. "Tell your pals. And I have a business proposition. Thought you might be interested."

"This better be good," says Big Nose.

"It is. I have the one gold coin I owe you, and I have a way for you to earn two more."

I take one of the coins out of my pocket and hold it down low, where only they can see it. Freckles makes a grab, but I'm too quick for him.

"Not so fast," I say. "You only get this one and two others if you agree to the deal."

"I think it's real," Freckles says. "Could be worth a fortune!"

"They're real, all right," I say. "And three of them are

yours—one now, and two when you get the job done. You want in?"

They want in. I tell them the plan, give them the one coin, and make my way back to our seat.

"Three minutes!" yells the conductor. "Camden Station next and final stop!"

It takes more like five minutes, but eventually the train comes into the station, and everyone gets off, including us. Hubie makes sure to stay exactly one half step behind us as we walk down the platform toward the gate.

"What's the next part of the plan?" Brandon whispers. "Don't we have to change a train someplace?"

"We have to change *stations*," I say. "That's what Tad said, remember? Something about the gauges."

"Right, the gauges," says Brandon. "So what are gauges?"

"The uh . . . you know. The gauges."

"It's the width of the rails, brainiacs," says Bev. "Didn't you guys ever play with toy trains? Different railroads had different gauges, meaning not all trains could run on all tracks. So I'm guessing we have to switch to a different station because they have different tracks and different trains."

"I had a computer game when I was like five years old," says Brandon. "Choo-Choo Charlie, I think it was called. But I never had an actual model train set."

"Let's focus," I say. "Tad said once we get to Camden Station, then we have to find the Bolton Station. And from there we can get a Northern Central train to Pennsylvania."

"And where's Bolton Station supposed to be?" says Brandon.

"In Bolton," Bev and I say at the same time.

"And what are we supposed to do . . . about our big friend?" Brandon says. "Is he going to just follow us around everywhere we go?"

"Not if my plan works," I say.

"What plan is this, Mel?" asks Bev.

"*The* plan. Which, if I've timed it right, should be starting right about now. When I say the word, run. And I mean run."

"Run?" says Brandon. "Run where?"

"Outside," I say, and then, behind us, Pimples, Freckles, and Big Nose come right up beside Hubie and frantically begin pointing backward. The second Hubie turns his head, I yell "Run!" and *four* of us follow instructions to the letter.

Four, when there should only be three.

Four of us run down the platform and through the gate, darting around every passenger in our way, then climb the stairs into Camden Station proper, which is crowded, smoky, noisy, hot, and dirty.

Four kids. Me, Brandon, and Bev, and Big Nose. And then I understand *their* plan—two of them, Freckles and Pimples, are going to tie up Hubie long enough for us to make our escape, while the third one, Big Nose, is going to make sure I pay up.

We run to the street outside the station. "We have a minute, maybe two," I say to Big Nose, reaching into my pocket for the two extra gold coins. "Do you know how we can get to the Bolton Station? Our next train leaves in thirty minutes."

"Why Bolton Station?" asks Big Nose. "Headed somewhere else?"

"Does it matter?" I say.

"Give me another one and I'll tell you," he says.

"What's going on, Mel?" Bev says. "Isn't this one of those . . . kids on the train?"

"Yeah," I say. "They've sort of agreed to help out."

"Didn't agree to nothin'," Big Nose says. "Just business, pure and simple. Now, you give me an extra coin and I'll show you the way to the Bolton Station. Otherwise, I just might go back and inform the gentleman where you're headed next."

"All right," I say, reaching into my pocket. "Which way?"

"Too far to walk," he says, "if you're fixing to catch another train in thirty minutes. You'll have to take a carriage. There they are—ask one of 'em to take you. Now give me the coins and I'll make sure we hold off your friend for another five minutes. After that you're on your own." He holds out his hand.

I fork over three coins. He snatches them and takes off back to the station.

"Let's go!" I say, and we run at full speed to the line of carriages that are rapidly being hired. We go up to the first one that's free.

"How much to Bolton Station?" I ask him.

"A dollar," he says.

"For three people?"

"Then two dollars," he says.

I give this guy one of my ten-dollar greenbacks. The carriage pulls out of the line and starts heading up the street, which is crowded with people carrying bags and luggage and hurrying around like an earthquake is about to happen. I kind of don't get why at first.

"What's the deal?" I say to the driver. "Where's everyone going?"

He turns around. "Out of town," he says. "Haven't you heard? The Rebs invaded Pennsylvania, smashed the Union Army, and are laying waste to everything in their path. Now they're on their way to Washington City. But first they're going to take Baltimore. It's going to get ugly around here, I promise you."

"Wait a minute," I say. "Today is July second, right?"

"Last I heard," says the driver.

"So who says the Rebs are marching to Baltimore? And have smashed to smithereens the Union Army?"

"Everybody," says the driver. "Look around."

"Guys," I say to Brandon and Bev. "I'm not sure about this."

"You're not sure about what?" says Bev.

"The dates. The Battle of Gettysburg happened over three days, right? July first, July second, and July third. Right?"

Brandon shrugs his shoulders. Bev snarls, "We're not history nerds like you, Mel. Maybe, maybe not. And your point is?"

"My point is, maybe all these people are just panicking. Wouldn't you? All they know is what they heard, which is that the Confederate Army marched into Pennsylvania. It's only logical to think what might happen next. But nobody knows the outcome, or even much of what's going on. President Lincoln himself told us he's getting very few reports. So people are just panicking. That's all it is."

I add, underneath my breath, two words I think I better keep to myself: *I hope.*

Our carriage turns right, heads up a dusty dirt road—the roads in Baltimore are even worse than the roads in Washington City—and things are more clogged up, more intense. People are shouting and pushing around each other and snarling in each other's faces.

"Right up there," the driver says. "Bolton Station. I'm not sure we're going to be able to get much closer."

The road is jammed now with other carriages trying to get to the Bolton Station, and along the side of the road, men, women, and children are hurrying along faster than the stuck carriages.

"We're going to have to get out," I say. "And make a run for it."

"Where you folks headed?" the driver says. "New York? Boston?"

"Gettysburg," we answer at once.

The driver looks at us like we're crazy. "Why in the world would you want to go to Gettysburg?" he asks. "Don't you children know that's where the war is?"

We jump out of the carriage. "That's exactly the point," I say, and then we take off, at full run, for the Bolton Station.

We don't stop for a second, or even bother to check our rear, to make sure no one's following.

Which, as it turns out, might have been a very good idea.

# TWENTY-THREE

THE BOLTON STATION IS, as far as train stations go, not very impressive. It's basically just a two-story wooden building, with about ten thousand people trying to get on a train and go somewhere—somewhere being anywhere but Baltimore.

Bev, per usual, takes charge of finding the ticket booth and buying three tickets—it costs us a handful of greenbacks, but that's better than forking over any more gold coins. We find the track, and then we realize something: most of the ten thousand or so people jamming the place are getting off the train we're trying to get on—it must have just pulled in. Everyone is in a great big hurry and carrying as much stuff as they can get their arms around. Bags, trunks, suitcases, you name it—people are hauling stuff around. It takes twenty minutes for the train to clear out enough for us to get aboard. The departing passengers are full of unhelpful advice, telling us General Lee and the Confederates are right up ahead. Finally we find ourselves a seat on the right side.

"What those people were saying can't be true," Bev says. "Can it, Mel?"

"No, of course not," I say. "These are the panickers. The ones who run first and ask questions later. And in order to make themselves not feel so bad about running, they have to make up stories. So it seems so much worse than it really is."

"You sure about that?"

"Sure I'm sure," I say, not so sure. "I know General Lee's army is big, but it's not that big. They're still in Gettysburg. Day Two. One more day to go. Neither side has won yet, let alone marched halfway to Baltimore."

"All aboard!" yells the conductor, walking down the aisle. "Baltimore to Harrisburg, stopping at Woodbury, Mount Washington, Relay, Riders, Lutherville, Timonium, Texas, Cockeysville, Ashland, Sparks, Monkville . . ."

This must be the local train, but it's the only one we could find that stops in Hanover. The car fills, the whistle blows, the conductor shouts, and we start to pull out.

Then, just before we really get going, I look out the window and see a man running on the platform.

A small man with a thin, wispy mustache, wearing dapper clothes and a bowler-style hat—I figure he's twenty-five, maybe thirty. He's carrying what looks to be a large suitcase, and he's in a great hurry to get on the train.

"We won't stop!" the conductor yells. "You better run harder if you want to make it!"

The man runs harder, and just before we pick up steam he heaves his suitcase in and then jumps aboard.

Just another guy on the train, right? So we should have absolutely no reason to think twice about him.

"Tickets!" yells the conductor, and starts his way down our aisle.

The young man with the suitcase enters our car, maneuvers around the conductor, and begins searching for a seat. He can't find one until he comes to us, and scoots in, without asking or receiving our permission. He hoists his suitcase above our heads to the coat rack, which he barely manages to do as the train jerks and hurtles along. But when he is finished, he sits next to Brandon, glances at each of us, and tips his hat.

"Aubrey Micawber," the man says. "At your service." He takes off his hat, and we see that he is well on his way to losing his hair. His skin is white—as in bone white—and he's smoking a small cigar, which stinks. "I'm the North American correspondent with the Manchester *Guardian*," he says, and thrusts his hand out. "Based out of Toronto, Canada." We hesitate, because this man seems almost friendly, unlike everyone else we've met so far.

"Well, are you going to shake or aren't you?" he says. "A fellow can't wait all day."

There's no reason—or at least no *apparent* reason—not to shake, so we do, and introduce ourselves.

"So," says Aubrey Micawber. "Where you headed, then?"

"Um, Pennsylvania, Mr. Micawber," Bev says.

"Please call me Aubrey," Aubrey says. "Mr. Micawber sounds so awfully . . . stuffy, don't you think?"

"All right," Bev says. "Aubrey, it is."

"Anywhere special in Pennsylvania?" he asks.

"No," I quickly say. I'm thinking of Mr. Hart's text, and his warning to beware of strangers. "Just Pennsylvania."

"Very well, then," he says. "Don't mean to pry."

To change the subject, Bev does a little prying herself. "So what do you do for the Manchester *Guardian*?" she asks.

"All depends on what the assignment is. I've had my fair share of political work—but honestly, the passage of a bill or the run-up to an election has more lows than highs. These days, of course, there is but one story from America that interests the Manchester *Guardian*—this war. Our readership is of two minds: they hate slavery, but they love money. And the current system has benefited the powers that be in Manchester, I can assure you of that. The textile mills are booming, and all the cotton is produced on Southern slave plantations. Or should I say the textile mills *were* booming, under the system that prevailed before this war. How this all gets sorted out, of course, is anyone's guess."

Brandon chimes in: "Where you headed?"

"Why, Gettysburg, Pennsylvania, young lad," says Aubrey. "My sources have informed me that a great battle is looming. I hope to get there before it's too late." He glances up at the suitcase on the rack above our heads. "Let me show you." He hauls down the suitcase, puts it on his lap, and opens it up. "I have everything I need right here." It's an old-fashioned camera setup. Well, not really old-fashioned—for 1863, it's probably the best they have.

"Oh," says Bev. "You're a photographer?"

"Photographer and writer, I'm afraid. The writing comes naturally, but the photography takes a bit of work. It obliges you to stay in one place for quite some time in order to get the shots, which is exactly the opposite of how I like to write a story—by moving around, figuring things out. But the *Guardian* of Manchester will not send two when they think one will do. Saves them a man's salary, which ought to go in my pocket but doesn't."

*Okay then,* I tell myself. *Just an ordinary correspondent from the Manchester* Guardian *who happened to board the train late, first of all, and then just happened to sit next to us.* I'm going to need to text Mr. Hart as soon as I get the chance.

This is the local train, so with all the herking and jerking, squealing wheels, and lurching stops, I'm starting to get a little queasy. Brandon? Forget about it. He's turned pale green, almost. If he has to hurl, he better not do it near me.

And then we cross into Pennsylvania. I know, because the conductor tells us. Not so much tells us as shouts it at us. "New Freedom, Pennsylvania!" he shouts. "New Freedom, Pennsylvania!"

I give Brandon a nudge. "Hear that?" I say. "New Freedom, Pennsylvania, next stop. We're getting close."

"I'm getting close." Brandon groans. "To puking on the floor. I'll never get on a train again as long as I live."

"We're not there yet, Brandon."

"I mean after this," Brandon whispers, so Mr. Aubrey Micawber won't be able to overhear us. "When we get back. Which will be when exactly, Mel?"

"Tomorrow, I think."

"Tomorrow?"

"Yeah."

"You sure?"

"Pretty sure. So long as the Union wins, we're good to go."

"And if they don't?"

"That would be a problem. If the Rebs win, that could be all she wrote. It would be the end of the United States, maybe. The whole country would be split it two, probably forever. And then who knows what would happen to anything, including us."

"I need a break from these trips," Brandon says. "The pressure's getting to me."

"Me too," I say.

We pull into New Freedom, PA. "Next stop will be Hanover Junction," shouts the conductor. "Hanover Junction, next stop!"

I get up, maneuver past Aubrey, and head to the front of the train, where I find an empty seat. Aubrey could have had it all to himself, I think, but for some reason chose to sit with us.

Weird.

I take out my phone, fire up. No incoming from Mr. Hart. I text: *On next leg. Due to arrive Hanover Junction 10 minutes.*

Less than a minute later he responds: *Secure?*

*Think so*, I say.

*Think so? Not sure?*

*Pretty sure.*

*YOU MUST BE 100% SURE, MEL!!!!!! Be suspicious of EVERY stranger!*

*Okay, I get it, as far as I know we're secure!*

*Text when you get closer. Imperative you arrive today!*

I power down. Mr. Hart might want to think about throwing in a nice word or two once in a while—*Hey, how are you?*—that kind of thing. Wouldn't hurt, and wouldn't cost a gold coin either.

I check my pocket, just to make sure: four coins left. They're going to have to last us through whatever we encounter ahead. I make my way back to the car. Only one problem: no Aubrey, no Brandon, and no Bev either.

# TWENTY-FOUR

There's no reason to panic. Or so I tell myself. Maybe they decided to stretch their legs and go for a stroll. Or use the facilities. Or get a bite to eat, if they have a food car on this train.

I'm sure there's a perfectly reasonable explanation, and what I ought to do is sit down and chill.

I sit. Aubrey's suitcase is back in the rack above our heads, and his jacket's on his seat. It's also a hundred and ten degrees inside the car. I look at his jacket, and I think: I should probably leave it alone. I have no business messing with it.

On the other hand . . . Mr. Hart did tell me to be suspicious of EVERY stranger. My hand—completely on its own, I swear—just then accidentally brushes Aubrey's jacket, causing it to fall to the floor. I have to pick it up, of course. And put it back where it belongs. Can I help it if my fingers glide along each and every pocket as I'm doing the guy a good deed?

There's something stuffed in the pocket inside the coat. I look up the car, down the car—no one's coming—undo the button, and extract a piece of paper. We can't be too sure, is my logic. Not when the future of the Union is at stake.

It's a telegram.

At the top it says, "AMERICAN TELEGRAPH CO., GENERAL OFFICE, 145 BROADWAY, NEW YORK."

Handwritten is the date—July 2, 1863—and the recipient: Aubrey Micawber.

Also handwritten is the message. "Baltimore," it says at the top. Then: "Mr. Micawber: we have reason to believe three young persons, two boys, one girl, 12 or 13 years old, may have boarded the Northern Central Line to Harrisburg. Destination unknown. As part of your duties with us you are directed to maintain close surveillance and if possible ascertain plans/destination/purpose. Report at earliest. Sincerely, JR, The Pinkerton Agency."

I stare at the telegram so I can commit to memory every word, then I fold it back just as it was and carefully return it to the inside pocket of Aubrey's coat.

First Hubie, now Aubrey. I take out my phone, text Mr. Hart. *Believe we are being followed. New person. Working for Pinkerton Agency.*

I don't tell him that this person hired by the Pinkerton Agency has also *disappeared* with Bev and Brandon, because, you know? Sometimes there's just no point in alarming somebody who can't do a thing about it.

Mr. Hart texts back: *Pinkerton Agency? What's up with that?*

*Kurtis must have hired them.*

*Them?*

*There was also this other guy, but we got rid of him.*

*So you ARE being followed!*

*Guess so.*

*NOT GOOD, MEL!!!! DON'T YOU REALIZE WHAT'S AT STAKE?*

Okay, stop yelling, Mr. Hart, I say to myself. And of course I realize what's at stake—just the fate of the Union.

*Got it*, I text back. *Will check back in 1 hour.*

Meanwhile, I need to locate Bev and Brandon, and pry them loose from the impostor, Aubrey Micawber.

I slide the door open to the front car again and step through. Union soldiers, dressed in blue. No Aubrey, no Bev. I turn around and head toward the rear of the train, checking each car as I go, and still no Aubrey and no Bev. In the last car, I take an empty seat. There has to be an answer, I tell myself. They just couldn't have disappeared off the face of the earth.

On the other hand—two days ago was 1776, and today is 1863, so I'm not going to be so quick to discount anything. Maybe Bev inadvertently activated her iTime app and all of them zoomed back to the Stone Age.

Ahead of me, the conductor enters the car and shouts, "Hanover Junction, next stop!" as loud as he can.

Then I hear—dimly, distantly—laughter. And not just any laughter: Brandon's. I'd recognize it anywhere.

I turn around. At the end of the last car is an outdoor platform, and there they are, the three of them, riding along, laughing it up like they're having the best time in the world.

I go out on the platform. "Found you guys," I say.

"Just enjoying the breeze," says Aubrey Micawber.

It's kind of nice, for a second. We're outside, we're rolling along, the wind is blowing in our hair. But then I remember our *mission*. And the inconvenient fact that this guy Aubrey is not exactly the innocent bystander he's pretending to be. I'm just about to say something when Brandon starts tugging on my sleeve, like he wants my attention, which is kind of annoying.

"What?" I say to Brandon.

Brandon points his finger to his right. "Look!"

I turn my head to see where he's pointing and what I see is not good.

Men in gray.

On horseback.

The Confederate cavalry.

And leading the charge is a long-haired dude with a goatee, waving around a huge sword above his head. And he's smiling, like he's having the time of his life. And I do believe he might even be whooping.

Which ought to be—but isn't—kind of like a major clue for the engineer to slam on the brakes.

"Stop the train!" I start yelling, to whoever will listen. "Stop the train before it's too late!"

It's too late.

The Confederate dude isn't just riding around to look good. He and his men have sabotaged the tracks.

Meaning they have blown up or wrecked somehow the very tracks we are riding on, and now they're waiting to witness the destruction.

It happens fast. One minute we're going along at thirty miles an hour. The next we have to stop before we hit a ditch.

The engineer slams on the brakes. But a train with five passenger cars can't exactly stop on a dime.

So it feels like we kind of move and stop at the same time, which, according to the laws of physics, doesn't work so well. Something's got to give.

I'm not even going to mention the noise. The whole screeching-crunching-twisting-metallic-braking noise is off the charts.

Finally we stop. Then we lurch backward, and we're all thrown every which way. I lose track of Bev, Brandon, Aubrey, the conductor, and everyone else. It is the ultimate survivor scenario. Every man, every kid, every girl, can only do one thing, and that is to somehow find a way to take care of your own self.

I'm not just thrown, I am *propelled*—like a rocket—through the air until I crash into the left side of the train, maybe two inches below the window. Had I hit the window, that would have been all she wrote for good old Mel. As it is, I even manage to get my arm up before my head hits. It hurts my arm, but saves my head.

Then I start tumbling over. I don't know if it's just me, or if it's just the car we're in, or if it's the whole train, but I know what falling feels like, and I'm falling through something or to something—it's not a hundred percent clear what's going on—and I land with a *thump* and a *thump* and a *thump*.

I think on solid ground.

I hear glass crashing all around. More terrific metal-screeching sounds. High-pitched screams blending into the mix.

Then it seems like a bunch of stuff starts landing on top of me, and at first I'm totally afraid, in fact I nearly panic, because I'm thinking, *Oh no, here it comes, the steel beams*—but no, it's not steel beams, it's stuff so light I almost laugh: Carpet bags. Fruit baskets. Newspapers. A ball of wool and a knitting needle.

Other than my arm, I'm all right. I can even get to my feet, once I push off all the debris that has landed on my back.

First thing I see is about twenty Confederate soldiers howling it up.

As if causing a train to stop dead in its tracks is a whole lot of *fun*.

Maybe for them it is. For us, not so much.

"Bev!" I yell. "Brandon! Where are you?"

There's no immediate answer, so I yell again, but louder.

Brandon was right next to me, so he can't be too far away, and Bev was on the other side of him.

"Bev!" I shout. "Brandon!" I try again, this time louder, which just adds to the overall noise and confusion, and keep at it until somebody yells right back at me. It takes a moment for me to register it, though. But this somebody keeps yelling till she comes through loud and clear.

It's Bev. I'd be happy to see her, except I finally get what she's yelling: "Mel! Hurry! It's Brandon! He's gone!"

**OLD SNAPPING TURTLE**

# TWENTY-FIVE

"**G**ONE WHERE?" IS THE first dumb thing out of my mouth.

"I don't know!" she says. "He's disappeared!"

Perhaps I give the impression that this information is not registering. Bev's manner of dealing with this condition is simple: she grabs me by my shirt and yells, "Mel! Do you hear what I'm saying? Brandon's *disappeared*! What are we going to do?"

"Why?" I say, because it's the only word that pops into my mind.

Bev shakes her head, but gives me the once-over. I think it's beginning to dawn on both of us that maybe I'm not one hundred percent *there* yet.

Uh, excuse me, but I've only just been in a

near-catastrophic train wreck. Which isn't something that happens every day. So I need a minute, okay? To orient myself.

To get a grip.

But it's not easy. I'm standing outside, looking at a train that has been practically upended. Luggage, clothes, hats, shoes, you name it, are scattered everywhere. People are walking up and down the train, rifles drawn, as if they're looking to take prisoners. . . .

Wait a minute.

People?

With rifles?

*Those aren't people,* my brain starts screaming at me. *Those are Confederate soldiers!*

"Bev!" I start. "We need to get out of here! Those guys over there are taking prisoners! They're Confederates! Let's run!"

I grab her by the arm and try to pull her away. "We can't, Mel!" Bev says. "We have to find Brandon! He's disappeared!"

"We can't help him from prison!" I answer, and we start running.

We see the flashy guy on horseback, the Confederate officer who seems to be in charge. He's still holding his long sword, and seems very pleased with himself. "Surrender yourselves!" he starts yelling. "Surrender yourselves to the Army of Northern Virginia and to the Confederate States of America!"

It seems we have an answer for him. Because those two hundred other people Bev and I happen to be running off with? They aren't just *people*, exactly.

Most of them are Union soldiers, on their way to the front.

Which means they are armed. And dangerous.

So they start to do what soldiers do. Which is to find themselves positions, like behind a tree or a wheelbarrow, load their rifles, and fire away.

I haven't seen this much fighting since Trenton. I think that was two days ago, in what would be real time for us.

Bev and I find our own tree to hide behind. Our guys are shooting at their guys, who are shooting back. The Confederate guys are on horseback, though, so they don't exactly stick around and take it. They gallop off to the other side of the train, which puts them out of range for the time being. Our guys stop firing, and all of a sudden it's very quiet.

Which gives me a good opportunity to get some things straightened out.

"Bev," I start. "Listen to me. That Aubrey guy is one of *them*."

"You mean he's a Confederate?"

"No. I mean he's with Kurtis."

"How could he be with Kurtis?"

"Kurtis must have hired him through the Pinkerton Agency. Same as Hubie was."

long-haired dude. "Drop 'em where we can see them, and come out of these woods with your hands in the air and your mouths shut!" He wheels his horse around and trots over to Bev and me, and lets Brandon slide off.

"Rufus T. Buford," he says, and gives us a crisp salute. "Captain, Cavalry Corps of the Army of Northern Virginia. Whatever may be said of us, we don't shoot women, children, or girls."

Captain Rufus T. Buford is by far the best-dressed officer I have ever seen. His gray uniform is pressed, cleaned, and has gold piping and gold buttons. On his shirt collar are three bars, and on his cuff is a fancy gold braid. His hair is very long, as is his goatee. His boots are jet black and well polished. And his long silver sword gleams in the sunlight.

"Well, that's good to know," Bev says. "You just nearly crashed a train that was carrying women, children, and girls. But you don't shoot them."

"Whoa, whoa, little missy," says Rufus T. Buford, smiling. "Don't you be getting your hackles up at me. This here is a war effort. And this here train was carrying war material and personnel, as you can plainly see. We had no way of knowing that children—and girls—would be on board. No way at all. So you make sure you mind your manners, young gal, or we'll round you up with the others. You hear me?"

"She's fine, Captain," says Brandon. "There'll be no problem here."

"Are sure about that, Mr. Brandon?"

"I'm sure, Captain Buford."

"I have your word?"

"You have my word," Brandon says.

"In that case, I bid you good day, and good luck. Now I have some prisoners to round up. Long live the Confederate States of America!" Captain Rufus T. Buford rises up on his horse, yells, and rides off.

"'Little missy'!" fumes Bev. "The nerve of that guy!"

"Brandon?" I say. "How exactly did you wind up with Captain Crazy Hair?"

"His name is Rufus T. Buford, Mel. And he's cool. Considering that he's a Confederate, that is."

"Okay, maybe, but how did you meet up with the guy?"

"Well, the train stopped, I was thrown out sideways, and I think I might have hit my head and blacked out for a minute or two. Next thing I know, I'm wandering around, looking for you guys, but I guess I must have gone in the wrong direction. I went toward *them*, not toward us. Meaning the Confederates. Actually, now that I think about it, I might have stumbled right *between* the Confederates and the Union guys. Into the crossfire. And then the next thing I know, Captain Rufus T. Buford is coming right at me. I mean, *right* at me, on his horse. Swinging his sword and everything. And he starts yelling at his own men to cease fire. Then he lifts me up to the back of his horse, and away we go."

"That's it?" I ask.

"That's it," Brandon says.

"So you're saying that the Confederate dude saved your life?"

"Pretty much."

"Terrific," says Bev. "Just terrific. So what are we supposed to do now?"

"We still need to get to Gettysburg," I say. "That hasn't changed. I don't think."

"And how far is that, Mel?"

"From here? We're just outside Hanover Junction. I'm not sure. Twenty miles maybe? Fifteen?"

"Wonderful. Why don't we just walk? That should be fun. But it fits in with everything else."

I'm about to agree with her. What other choices do we have, except to walk the whole way?

Then I hear, not too far away, what sounds like a bunch of barnyard animals.

Donkeys, braying as loud as they possibly could.

You know the sound—*hee-haw, hee-haw, hee-haw.* It sounds like they're agitated about something.

"What the . . . ," says Bev. She points her fingers to the road. We see, a hundred or so yards away, not only three real donkeys, but also two horses, four mules, carts, wagons, and a long double line of ladies.

You heard me right.

*Ladies.* Not soldiers. Not men or boys. Ladies, or maybe I should say *women,* though they really do look like ladies to me.

Each one is wearing a long black or brown dress, and,

of course, a hat. Even though it's July and a hundred and two degrees.

And each one is walking very determinedly and, I'd say, also very *properly*. No slouching, no shuffling. One foot in front of the other. No one is paying any attention to the braying donkeys they have with them.

"Where in the world do they think they're going?" Bev asks. "To church?"

"They're not bringing all that to church," Brandon says. "They look like they're going someplace on purpose."

"Yeah," I say. "Like they have a *mission*." I start to notice more details—each donkey and mule is hauling a cart, piled high with trunks, satchels, and lots of other packed-up stuff. And two or three additional women ride on each one of the carts, in as ladylike a fashion as they can manage.

No one is smiling, or attempts to get the donkeys to shut up. Instead they keep walking, at the same steady pace, until the lady at the head of the line brings the company to a halt. They're only about fifty yards away from us now. We can clearly see them, and they can clearly see us.

"You, children!" the lead lady shouts over. "Come here this instant!"

I know right away that this isn't going to go well—Bev is a live wire and Brandon is a loose cannon, and neither of them are going to mix with a few dozen proper *ladies*—but we trot over there anyway.

This lead lady is tall, broad-shouldered, full in the face,

immediately to General Meade's headquarters. He's in overall charge of the army."

"General Meade? Old Snapping Turtle? He's the meanest man I ever met. Ain't no way I'm bringing you to him. He'd swipe my head off for even thinkin' on it."

"Maybe, but we need to see him."

"You think I'm going to let you through just like that? Put my hide on the line? Ain't no man under the rank of full colonel wants to go near General Meade, and I'd wager even a full colonel's knees go a-tremblin' when they do so. Every man knows it, right down to their bones. You don't mess with Old Snapping Turtle. Better the Rebs than him."

"Well, be that as it may, we have business with him. If you can't take us there, point us in the right direction."

"I hate to break this to you, but we are in the middle of a war. Captain Toland told us he never seen nothin' like it, and hopes never to see worse, but suspects he might before the whole thing is over. You best be served to go back the way you come and wait for another time. Now move along, because you're jammin' up the road. I still got troops coming through."

"Listen, you," says Bev. "Last night we had dinner with Mr. and Mrs. Lincoln. The president himself gave us a special message to deliver in person to General Meade. Now, you either let us through or you're going to be in big trouble, mister."

"I ain't got the time to waste with you," the lieutenant says. "Go back the way you came."

Our protests are not heard, and the gathered groups behind us press ahead, petitioning the lieutenant for entrance. We shuffle off to the side to let the hordes pass.

"Now what?" says Bev.

"We are going to have to come up with something," I say, noticing the steady stream of men, horses, carts . . .

Carts . . .

"Hurry," I say, running about twenty yards down the road. I see a covered cart being hauled along by a team of young soldiers, barely older than us. "We've come to fight," I tell them, "but they won't let us by. I'll give you a gold coin if you let us ride in the back."

"And where you be headin'?" is the only thing he asks of us.

"To General Meade's headquarters," I tell him. "It should be right in the middle of everything."

"What you want to go there for?" the boy says. "You got business?"

"You bet we do," I say. "Now, you want this or what?"

The head boy takes the gold, jerks his head, and we crawl in the back of the cart and throw a tarp over our heads just in time to pass by the lieutenant, undetected.

Which only proves that if you're really, really determined to do something, you can do it.

Just better hope that it's a smart thing to do. At this point it's too late to turn tail and run.

# TWENTY-NINE

THIS CART WE'RE IN is maybe as big as two wheel-barrows. I'm to the right, then Bev, then Brandon. Think of three sardines in a can. Maybe in theory I wouldn't mind being next to Bev, but in reality?

Puhleeze. I tell her to stop moving around. She tells me to shut up. I tell her to get her elbow out of my ear. She tells me to pipe down. I tell her to stop kicking me, to stop kneeing me, and to cover her mouth when she sneezes. Especially when she's like two inches away from my face. She says, "Just be quiet," "Leave me alone," and "Bug off."

Boy, would I like to. You don't know how much I'd love to rip off that ratty tarp covering us and get out of this cart and walk to where we're going like a normal human being.

But no. The Chief Boy hauling us won't allow it.

"It's not far," he says, flipping the tarp cover over so he can talk to us. "We're cutting over from the Baltimore Pike to Taneytown Road. Twenty minutes at the most. I've asked around, they tell me you need to go to Cemetery Hill, where General Meade has his headquarters. Now, be quiet the rest of the way."

Everything worsens the closer we get—by now we're suffocating, we're sore, we're smelly, and we're unhappy. The smell that's getting stronger by the foot isn't the cart or the tarp or people or mules; it's the gunpowder. And the sounds are cannon blasts and rifle shots.

We *really* are going to battle.

The biggest battle ever fought on American soil. The battle that's *supposed* to decide the future of the Civil War, and thus the fate of our nation.

Now, if you ask me—and I've had some time to think this Civil War thing through—here's my take: the South basically said goodbye to the United States. Said, *We'll form our own country, and we'll run it our own way.*

*So see you later. Goodbye and good luck.*

My two cents is that dividing the U.S. in two for all time and forever doesn't seem like a great idea.

President Lincoln agreed. He told the South what he thought of their idea to leave the union. He told them: *No chance. Once in, always in. That's how it is, and like it or not, that's how it's gonna be. We wouldn't have a serious country if every time this state or that state got peeved over something, they decided to jump ship.*

But I don't think either side really expected a civil war like this one to be the upshot. . . .

"Are you talking to yourself, Mel?" Bev asks.

"Leave me alone, Bev."

"I wish I could. But you're mumbling in my ear."

"Leave me alone, will ya? I was just thinking, that's all."

"Quiet in there!" says the Chief Boy. "I'm supposed to be transporting goods, not people, and the last time I checked, goods don't talk to one another!"

A *huge* explosion just then rattles our world, and even shakes our cart a little from side to side. We start tilting, and I almost fall overboard. Bev makes sure to stick her knees and elbows into me as hard as she can.

But the cart is righted and we continue on our way. "Not to worry about that," says the Chief Boy. "It was loud, but quite far away indeed. I do, however, believe we'll arrive at headquarters in about five minutes."

And then he adds, "If all goes well."

I wish he hadn't said that.

Because five minutes later nothing goes well. Our cart gets knocked over, we tumble out of it and into a puddle of mud, and a troop of passing soldiers yell at us for getting in their way.

We scramble out of the mud and out of the way. We're kind of on an upslope. And we are by no means isolated. In fact, there are so many people—by *people* I mean soldiers—around us that it's almost as claustrophobic as being in the cart under a blanket next to Bev. I feel like a thousand pairs of eyes are watching our every move. They're watching in little groups of threes and fours. Scattered kind of everywhere across the fields are little campfires, which emit a soft glow that shine on grim, dirty faces.

To our left, on the other side of the Taneytown Road, is a little white house. Maybe at one time it was freshly painted and had a nice picket fence around it, and in front a garden full of ripe tomatoes and lovely flowers.

That time is not this time. The picket fence is busted to pieces, the grounds are trampled to mud and dirt, and there are big holes in the roof and bullet holes all over the side of the house.

And it's the only building on the meanest battlefield of all time.

Bev is peeved from landing in the mud. She tries to brush herself off, but it only makes things worse. Brandon doesn't care about the mud, but he crinkles his nose—we don't smell gunpowder so much as we do bacon. Some of the men are using the campfires to cook themselves dinner, which reminds all of us, but especially Brandon, that we've gone the whole day without eating a thing.

I take out my phone, check in. I've got a text from Mr. Hart. *Meade's HQ is a small white farmhouse on the edge of Cemetery Hill. It's called the Leister Cottage. Ask around if you must. As for Kurtis, he is shortish and somewhat overweight. He may be dressed in disguise, but he will not be able to hide his dimensions.*

"No way," I say.

"What?" says Bev.

"That," I say, pointing to the run-down farmhouse in front of us, "cannot be General Meade's headquarters."

"Then what are all those generals doing?" Brandon asks. "There must be a dozen of 'em, maybe more. Looks like they're heading inside."

Brandon is correct. The men all have Union blue uniforms with gold bars on their shoulders, and each one of them looks every inch the general.

"And we do what now?" says Bev. "Look for a short overweight guy?"

Before I can think it through, a man comes walking toward us from out of the darkness. He has his hands folded behind his back. He is also wearing a blue uniform, and has gold bars on his shoulders. He stops, noticing us.

"You are children," he says.

"We are, sir," I say.

"Your ages?"

We tell him.

"Your names?"

We tell him that as well.

"Whatever shall happen here," he says, "this night, on the morrow, for the duration of this war—you will reap it. We will either be one nation, as our forefathers envisioned, or we will not. We have come to the crisis point. I have taken a solitary walk, as is my custom, before this meeting with my War Council. I have little doubt each of my generals will voice his views and his stratagems to the utmost. But what say you? For what we do in the next few hours will have far greater impact on you and your generation than on any of us. We are old, we have lived our lives; whether we succeed or fail, our years are short. Speak your mind, young ones. Have no fear of me."

The man is kind of bug-eyed, he's got a high forehead and an atrocious comb-over job, a shaggy gray beard, and his uniform could use a little spiffing up. But I have a pretty good idea who he is.

"Are you General Meade, sir?" I ask.

"I am indeed," he says. "Although I have been given a nickname, I fear. The men snicker when they say it, thinking I have no ears to hear them. Do you know it?"

"No, sir," I say.

"No?" he asks, a very slight smile crossing his very thin lips. "Perhaps you are too kind to say it aloud. They call me Old Snapping Turtle. It is true, I have lost my temper on occasion. I have yelled, I have barked, and I have let my displeasures be known. But I assure you, for all my faults, and I certainly have as many as any man, my temper is the least of them. History will care not about my temperament or my disposition; history will care solely about my judgment. And so I ask you again: what say you?"

"About what exactly, General Meade?" Bev says.

"About our decision, of course," he says. "This is why

we are having a Council of War. We must decide if we should stay here and fight another day, or retreat to safer ground while we have the chance."

"But . . . General Meade!" I say. "You can't retreat! You just can't! It's not how it's supposed to go!"

"'Supposed to go,' young man? Whatever does that mean? We were not 'supposed' to have a civil war, were we? We were 'supposed' to have a perpetual union of like-minded states, were we not? That banded together under the belief that the benefits of unity would forever be greater than the disadvantages of conformity. That is what we were 'supposed' to be about, young man. That ideal has likely been shattered forever. But at least in order to save ourselves, I shall propose to my Council of War that we begin our retreat forthwith. Thank you. You have assisted me in making up my mind."

A young officer approaches us. "General Meade," he says. "We were worried—not sure where you'd gotten off to."

"A walk is all it was," General Meade tells him. "A solitary walk does wonders. Then I came across my young friends here. They have helped me clarify my thoughts, to a good end. Now I must bid you good night. My generals await me."

He nods his head, but as he is led back to his head-quarters by the young officer, Bev can't help herself. "You can't retreat, General Meade!" she blurts out. "You can't just run away. General Lee will track you down."

"It's a chance I am willing to take, young lady. Now, as I said, my generals await. I would hope you will go the way you came. It is most dangerous here. Most dangerous indeed, for all of us."

Bev isn't done. "And what do we think history will make of this? They'll say you turned and ran."

"Perhaps. If I save my army, then perhaps not. In either case, history doesn't have General Lee and ninety thousand Confederate soldiers to contend with—I do." And then Old Snapping Turtle—who hadn't snapped at all—turns his back on us and walks into the ramshackle house that is serving as his headquarters.

And I am left with a very terrible feeling.

It starts right in my gut and radiates outward, to my feet and fingers and head, at warp speed.

Somehow *we* have become the outside force. The outside force that changes the sequence of events at the Battle of Gettysburg, and thus the course of history for all time to come.

# THIRTY

"So *we're* THE ENEMY?" says Brandon, after I explain my theory. "How can that be?"

"Don't you see? If we hadn't showed up, General Meade would never have decided to retreat."

"Boys," says Bev. "Don't get yourselves in a tizzy. He had already decided. It wasn't us. Something else is going to happen. I am one hundred percent positive."

"Oh yeah, Bev?" I say. "What makes you so sure?"

"I have a feeling."

"A feeling?"

"That's right. And we can't stand around and look at one another. What's the plan, Mel?"

"The first part of the plan was to get here, which we've done. The second part was to find Kurtis, which we haven't done. I'm going to check in." I text Mr. Hart: *At Meade's HQ. No sign of K. Meade's planning to retreat, by the way.*

Barely five seconds go by before I get his return blast: *KURTIS IN VICINITY!!!!!! FIND HIM!!!!*

"Mr. Hart is getting to be pretty annoying," Brandon says. "Should we just put up a sign—'Dear Kurtis, Please Report to Reception'?"

"No, it should say 'Please Report to HQ,'" says Bev.

"Let's fan out," I say. "If he's in the vicinity, he's in the vicinity, right? We need to think this out. If you were Kurtis, what would you do?"

"You're telling me all the Union generals are gathering to have a Council of War?" Brandon says, nodding to General Meade's run-down headquarters.

"Of course," Bev says. "That's why Kurtis is up here, isn't it? It's all about the generals."

"We need to get a peek inside," I say.

"How we going to do that, Mel?" says Brandon.

"There's always a way," I answer. "Where there's a will."

We circle the house, slowly, trying not to draw too much attention to ourselves, which isn't hard—no one pays attention to unarmed kids, especially on a battlefield. Guards at the front of the house block the door, but other than that we're pretty much free to roam around.

There are no guards at the back of the house.

But there are two small windows. Bev and Brandon peer through one, and I peer through the other.

The generals are gathered in a small, plain room. There must be ten or twelve of them. In the back is a little bed, and off to the side is a table at which three or four of the generals are seated. General Meade is standing, as is another general, who looks fitter and stronger than the rest. His beard is a very bushy goatee, and he, along with many others, is smoking a cigar.

"Do they have to smoke those things?" whispers Bev, waving her arm in front of her nose. "They are the worst-smelling things ever!"

"Shhh," says Brandon.

"Don't you shush me, Brandon," Bev says. "Who do you think you are?"

Brandon gives Bev a nudge, and she quiets down, at least for the moment. The generals continue talking, basically in small groups of twos and threes, and no one seems in any particular hurry to get the meeting started. Finally General Meade clears his throat and takes charge.

The other men fall silent. "Gentlemen," he says. "Our position here is unfavorable. This place is called Cemetery Hill. It serves its purpose, which is to accept the dead and let them lie in peace. It is not for armies to fight upon. I put before you the following proposition: Should our army remain on this field and continue the battle tomorrow, or should we move to some other position, such as Pipe Creek, Maryland? Our position there is fortified, reinforced, and impregnable."

"They'll go around the room," I whisper. "Beginning

with the most junior officer. It is the custom of the military."

We watch as the most junior officer stands up, waits for his comrades to quiet, and then speaks. "I say, correct our position if we must. But do not retreat."

"Stay," is all the next general says, and the two generals after him agree. The next one stands up and waffles around a bit before saying that he too thinks the army should stay and fight.

So it goes. No one agrees with Meade; they all want to stay and fight. Finally the general who is young and fit and has a bushy goatee takes the floor.

"I think that's General Hancock," I whisper. "He's basically the hero of Gettysburg. I mean he *will* be. Hopefully."

"Let us have no more retreats," General Hancock says. "Our army has had too many retreats . . . let this be our last retreat."

The next general stands up, nods appreciatively at General Hancock, glares at General Meade, and says simply, "Stay and fight."

The voting is done, and it is unanimous. General Meade does not look pleased, but these are not men he can simply snap at and order around. "Have it your way, gentlemen," he says. "But Gettysburg is no place to fight a battle. I will say this: if Lee attacks tomorrow, it will be at the center of our line. Mark my words. Because he has made attacks on both our right and left flanks and failed, and if he concludes to try again, it will be on our center."

And there it is.

The decision has been made. The battle—the battle of all battles—will be fought the following day. So we did *not* ourselves change anything to the contrary, as I feared. All is going, up till now, precisely as it is supposed to go.

So I guess we can all relax, right?

Then I notice something. In the corner of the room, underneath the bed.

A bag.

A black leather bag.

It has the initials T.G.W., INC. stenciled on the side.

# THIRTY-ONE

I'T'S FUNNY HOW TWO completely different things can happen at *exactly* the same time, but still be totally related. Like now. I see one thing, Brandon sees another.

Ever though it's dark outside, the room itself is bright with gas lamps. I can clearly see a black bag under a table. So naturally my mind goes down a certain road—bag, generals, T.G.W., Inc. Two plus two plus two equals bomb in the bag, right? To blow the whole command structure of the Union Army to pieces the night before the most important battle of the war. Blow us to pieces too, seeing as how we're practically standing next to the thing. That's what I'm thinking, anyway.

Brandon? He wasn't, it turns out, peering quite as intently inside the house as I was, or as Bev was. He got distracted, he'll tell us later. Kind of bored. So instead of looking in, he looked out. And what he sees is what he wants to tell me. So he taps me on the shoulder.

"Mel," Brandon says, "I think that's that guy we met on the train. Aubrey Whatshisname."

I follow Brandon's pointing outstretched finger: sure enough, it's our train friend Aubrey Micawber standing not twenty yards away from us. He of the Manchester *Guardian* and/or the Pinkerton Detective Agency.

"What's he doing here?" Bev says.

"I guess he survived the train," Brandon says.

"Look at this," I say. "Do you guys see that bag inside there? The black one under the bed?"

"Hold on, Mel," says Bev. "Who's that guy he's talking to?"

"You mean that short, overweight guy next to him?" says Brandon. "A Union soldier, right?"

Not right. "What's that soldier guy got in his hand?" I say. "And why's he looking at the house?"

And then all three of us see and think *exactly* the same thing at *exactly* the same time.

That's not any ordinary soldier dressed in Union blue.

Our biggest clue is that he's holding a phone just like ours.

Then I know. The recognition hits me like a punch in the gut. It's Kurtis himself, co-inventor of the iTime app and president of T.G.W., Inc. Aubrey Micawber is talking into his ear, pointing at the house, and Kurtis is tapping away on his phone.

"I have to get the bag," I say to Brandon and Bev. "Now! I think Kurtis is setting a bomb to go off. You guys should run. Wish me luck!"

I start running to the front, and I see Kurtis tap his phone for a final time, smile, and start to back away himself. Just before he does, our eyes meet and lock: he recognizes me, and sees where I'm heading. He nods his head once, then starts running away as fast as his short fat legs will carry him, and Aubrey Micawber follows behind.

How long until this blows? Two minutes? One?

I guess I should say a few words appropriate to the occasion. To my dad, I'd like to thank him for being—well, I kind of wish he wasn't *quite* so hard-charging and in-your-face and forward-leaning and get-it-done-nowish, but Dad is Dad, and there's nothing I'm going to do to change him at this point. But anyway, thanks, Dad, thanks for everything, I know you'd give pretty much anything you have to me, except some of your time, and I know, time is money, and money makes the world go round, but still. And Mom—well, I really kind of wish you hadn't decided to leave Dad, because you couldn't change him either but I'm sure Dad was Dad when you first met and decided to marry him, so I'm not sure what you expected then or what you expected later—but anyway, thanks for the mom-type stuff you did do when you lived with us, which was before I was shipped out to the Fredericksville School.

To our teacher Mr. Hart, all of this might be your fault, but I'm not really going to blame you, because after all, when we traveled back to 1776, it was an accident, but this time we knew what we might be getting into. This time we *chose*. So our fate is on us. I wish you luck, Mr. Hart, I do. You might want to find yourself some friends, though. A girlfriend even. You don't want to be the only teacher next year who has no place to go over the Christmas holidays.

Brandon? We've been through thick and thin. This will be the worst of it, though. It's sad, that it comes down to this. You're a much better person than I gave you credit for. You're not just a dopey loser dude, and I'm sorry if I ever thought you were. Peace out, bro.

And then we come to Bev. Bev, the one thing I'm sure of is that right now you're not thinking about me. And that's kind of the problem in a nutshell. Our relationship is *unequal*, Bev. Everything you do registers with me, and nothing I do registers with you. I'm just one half of this blobby entity you call "boys." And you know what? I don't think that's the right basis for a healthy relationship.

That's right, Bev. *Relationship*. You might not have noticed, but we have one. You and me. We've been thrown *together*, remember? Did you ever think, maybe for a reason?

I bet you haven't. I bet it never occurred to you for a single second.

And speaking of single seconds, I'm afraid that's about all we have left.

I rush past the guards posted outside General Meade's headquarters.

I open the door.

This might not be good.

It could even be *loud.*

This could go: *boom!*

General Meade's headquarters are full of foul-smelling cigar smoke and Union generals.

And Old Snapping Turtle goes off, but good. His face is red as an apple, his neck veins are throbbing thick ropes of rage, and spittle collects on his scraggly gray beard.

That kind of mad.

I think he might have forgotten that fifteen minutes ago we had a more or less pleasant conversation outside. No yelling, at least. Now he earns his nickname.

"WHAT IN THE WORLD ARE YOU DOING HERE? WHO GAVE YOU PERMISSION TO ENTER MY HEADQUARTERS? I WILL HAVE YOU ARRESTED AND COURT-MARTIALED!"

"I understand, sir," I say. "Believe me, I do. It's just that I think I left something behind. That bag over there. Underneath the bed." I skirt along the room before either General Meade or one of his underlings can react. I have to go through a big cloud of cigar smoke to get to where I need to go, and if the bag goes off now, my very last thought will be *Why in the world would anybody smoke a cigar in the first place?*

"STOP RIGHT THERE!" yells General Meade.

"ANYTHING IN THIS ROOM IS GOVERNMENT PROPERTY!"

"Everything except this," I say, grabbing the bag and hustling to the door. "See?" I point to the stenciled initials T.G.W., INC. "It belongs to this guy outside. He asked me to get it for him. It's the photography bag. I'm the assistant. To Mr. Aubrey Micawber of the Manchester *Guardian.*"

"HAVE YOU LOST YOUR MIND? GET OUT OF HERE! GET OUT OF HERE AND TAKE THAT . . . THAT BAG WITH YOU! I NEVER WANT TO SEE YOUR FACE AGAIN! I WILL HAVE YOU SHOT IF I DO!"

The other generals find General Meade's outburst amusing, but thankfully none of them make a move to stop me.

"OUT!!! NOW!!!"

I scamper through the cigar cloud and through the door, the bag gripped in my right hand. I *really* won't be happy if the thing blows now. As a matter of fact, I'm starting to get nervous.

As in panicky nervous.

As in scared-out-of-my-pants nervous.

I spot Bev and Brandon, who are maybe thirty yards away. Safe. Maybe.

"What should I do with it?" I say.

"You got to put it someplace," Bev says.

"Follow me," Brandon says, taking off. "I think there's a good spot down the road."

Brandon starts sprinting. Bev is right behind him.

I go as fast as I can, holding the bag, and I keep going until I can barely see the road or my feet. Then I hear Brandon.

"Mel! Right here! Toss it into the field!"

There are no soldiers, no generals, no auxiliary nurses anywhere nearby, so it's not a bad spot. If it goes kablooey and nobody gets hurt and nothing falls down, what's the harm?

None.

I toss it.

Then I run for my life.

# THIRTY-TWO

As far as bombs go—and it's not like I'm an expert or anything—when this one blows it's kind of so-so on the impressive meter.

I mean, how many things have I seen blown up? On TV, I mean, or in movies, I must have seen a thousand explosions. Two thousand. And pretty much each goes like this: a huge, ear-splitting blast, a rumble of the earth, a mountain's worth of fire and ash bellowing upward to the sky.

I make it to where Bev and Brandon are, we all huddle together, stick our fingers in our ears, wince our eyes shut . . . and . . . and . . . and then it goes *beep*.

Not *boom*.

No billowing plumes of fire and ash. More a burp than a blast.

"That's it?" asks Bev. "We risked our lives for that?"

"Maybe there's more to it," I say. "Poison gas or something?"

"That would have been a dumb way to do it," Brandon says. "All those generals could have had time to run out of the house if it was poison gas."

"Well, maybe we're missing something," I say. "But I'm pretty sure it was a bomb. Just didn't go off on time, and it was a dud. So maybe Kurtis isn't as all-powerful as we thought. He saw me, you know. When he was talking to Aubrey Micawber, he looked up and our eyes met. So he knows exactly where we are, and what we're doing. I better check in."

I take out my phone, power up. No messages from Mr. Hart. I start to type something in when I get an incoming.

But from a number I don't recognize, and isn't in my contacts list.

*Well, that was disappointing, wasn't it?*

"Who's sending this?" Brandon says.

"Who do you think?" says Bev.

"Should I say something back?" I say.

"I think you should text Mr. Hart," Bev says. "Let him know the situation."

I finish my message to Mr. Hart and hit Send but nothing happens. I hit it again, same result.

Then another incoming.

*No need to be shy.*

Followed by another: *The thing about technology? Sometimes it works and sometimes it doesn't. That was supposed* to be a much bigger blast, and of course it didn't go off when I wanted it to. But then again—first time I tried making a bomb. It usually takes me a few tries before I figure things out. You wouldn't believe what we had to go through to get the iTime app to work.

"I'm not liking this so much," I say. "Is he watching us from somewhere?"

"Probably," Bev says. "Let's answer him. We can tell him to stuff it."

That's as good a message as any to send, so I type it in.

*Nice,* he sends back. *Although if I were in your shoes I'd watch my manners. And you were warned. You should have gone home when you had the chance.*

*What for? So you could blow up General Meade?*

*I thought a bomb blast right in his HQ would be kind of spectacular, but win some, lose some. I wouldn't bet against me next time—I always have alternate plans. I'd put my chances at 97%.*

*97% to do what? Destroy the Union? Let the Confederate States of America keep slavery intact?*

*No. To prove that I am right and everyone else is wrong. History CAN be changed. History WILL be changed. You shall see. But I can tell you what you will not see, and that is your home.*

We can't even think of something to say back—we're still processing the fact that we'll never see our friends, our parents, our school—nothing—ever again.

But Kurtis is having too much fun to stop now. *I*

*understand your imaginations are limited, so hear me well: The Union will not prevail upon this battlefield tomorrow. With my assistance, in one week's time—if my calculations hold true—General Lee and his army will arrive on the outskirts of Washington, and Lincoln will be obliged to sue for peace. That will mean the end of this war. So you could say I am a force for good, no?*

*No,* I type. *You are not good now and you never will be.*

*Perhaps you are not yet able to perceive my genius. In fact, I'm growing a touch weary of merely altering history—that objective seems too easy now, even with you three getting in the way. I'm beginning to think I should go after something far grander: CREATING history! So I say unto you: watch, and behold!*

I turn off my phone. "He's crazy," I say. "Absolutely stark raving mad."

"What are we going to do, Mel?" asks Brandon.

"I have no idea," I say. I'm heading straight for the bag that might have blown up the entire Union command, but didn't. Or should I say what's left of the bag. Bits and pieces of leather are scattered around. Papers from inside the bag are scattered all over.

"Wow," I say. "Look at this." I pick up a piece of paper from the ground. "He's using stationery from the Gettysburg Hotel. Maybe that's where he's hanging out."

"Forget it, Mel," Bev says. "We're not going there."

"Why not? Got a better idea? Because we have the rest of 1863 to think of something better."

"You think all we have to do is to traipse across the battlefield, avoid the entire Confederate Army, enter town, find the Gettysburg Hotel, and fix everything?" Bev asks. "And all this in the dead of night?"

"I figure it shouldn't be a problem," I say. "Seeing as how we're all so, you know. Unified."

Except that we're not. Bev wants to stay put. Brandon wants to go right. And I want to go forward.

Bev's argument is that we haven't had a good night's sleep since 1776.

Brandon wants to find the Southern New Jersey Nurses' Auxiliary, wherever they may be, and throw our lot in with them. He very much admires Mrs. Harriet Claiborne, he tells us. She's the most sensible person he's met since . . . since he doesn't know when.

It's all becoming a little foggy. We're having trouble hanging on to our own line of reasoning. You've heard of jet lag, but let me tell you, it's got nothing on time-travel lag. You don't know tired until you've zipped back and forth across a century or two.

"I'm going to sleep," Bev says. "You two work it out. Let me know. In the meantime I am going to lie down right here. Look—a patch of grass." Then Bev—our Bev, mind you, the one with the Hollywood mom and the aspirations to cure cancer and Make the World a Better Place—lies down.

And closes her eyes. Soon she has a big fat smile on her face, as if she's in the world's fanciest hotel.

Speaking of hotels—there's one awaiting us. It's maybe a mile or two away. Nothing stands between us and it other than forty or fifty thousand soldiers.

But before I can stop him, Brandon lies down on the grassy patch next to Bev, makes himself comfortable, folds his hands under his chin, closes his eyes, and falls asleep.

Which leaves me.

On that grassy patch, right next to my fellow Left Behinds.

And Bev is right: it is pretty comfortable here.

Maybe I could just lie down for a second.

Before I go forth and Save the World and all.

I lie down.

I'll rest five, maybe ten minutes before I get up and reconnoiter the place, find the quickest way to town.

But first let me just close my eyes. . . .

An hour later, or two hours later, or maybe even three hours later, I'm half awakened. I'm dimly aware of someone standing over us, an old man in a worn Union blue uniform, with a high forehead, an atrocious comb-over, and a gray beard. General Meade throws blankets over each one of us, and then he's gone.

**THE BLUE, THE GRAY,
AND GENERAL ROBERT E. LEE**

# THIRTY-THREE

WE ARE AWAKENED, AT dawn's early light, by the movement of troops.

Thousands of them. Thousands and thousands and thousands. The Union Army is coming alive.

It is Friday, the third of July. 1863. Tomorrow will be July Fourth, eighty-seven years since the Declaration of Independence. Or, if you want to get all flowery about it, four score and seven years ago. That's what President Lincoln will say a few months from now, when he dedicates the cemetery, if he takes Brandon's suggestion.

Will say, that is, if everything goes according to plan, which at this very moment is kind of a big question mark. Kurtis has a whole day ahead of him to find a way to mess things up. As far as I can tell, we—Brandon,

Bev, and I—are the only ones that can do anything about it.

Not that anyone's paying much attention to three kids along the side of the road, though. We sit up, rub our eyes, and stare in wonder.

We haven't even seen this place properly before now. It was already nighttime when we arrived with the Southern New Jersey Nurses' Auxiliary, and we couldn't see any farther than the most distant reach of a torchlight.

"Holy smokes," says Brandon, stretching, yawning, scratching. "Where are we again?"

"We are in the middle," I say. "Smack-dab in the middle."

"In the middle of what?" he says.

"In the middle of the battlefield. I'm not sure this is the place we want to be, either."

"You think, Mel?" says Bev.

"We better get out of here," I say. "And fast. Today is the last day of the battle. Pickett's Charge and all that, right?"

"Pickett's Charge?" says Brandon. "What's that about?"

"It's about this dude named Pickett," I say. "He charged, but he shouldn't have. Got wiped out. Man, I bet that didn't even happen too far from where we are now. I mean—I bet that's *gonna* happen. Not too far from where we are now."

"Boys," says Bev. "You can talk it out all you want. Me, I'm finding someplace safer." She gets up, dusts herself off. "Um, which way you think that Pickett guy is going to be charging from? 'Cause I think maybe I want to go the other way."

I stand up beside her. In front of us and to the left is Old Snapping Turtle's headquarters. Soldiers, officers, orderlies are coming and going, everyone busy, in a hurry. Troops are marching right by us, on the dirt-packed Taneytown Road, which at this point inclines upward. I think they must be fresh troops, reinforcements sent from some other battle area or maybe just late arrivals. They look clean, relatively speaking. No blood, no torn uniforms, no one wounded. "I think we should fall in behind these guys," I say. "Maybe they're heading where we want to go."

"Which is where, exactly, Mel?" Bev says.

"Away from here. And into town. And that's where we need to go."

"Sounds too simple."

"You have any better ideas?"

"I ought to," Bev says. "I really ought to."

"Well, in the meantime, let's fall in," I say. And then we start walking behind the last line of troops in front of us, up the Taneytown Road.

The soldiers of the Union Army don't walk quietly. Rifles, canteens, and backpacks make a huge clicking-clacking noise, and their boots pound the ground with each step. As we walk up the incline, I can immediately see the main battlefield is going to be to our left.

It's basically a huge meadow that slopes down for a couple of miles until it ends in a forest. Where we are on the Taneytown Road is almost at the apex of the whole deal. The *high ground*, which, if I've learned anything from watching the History Channel so much, is always the most valuable real estate.

So the Union Army, including us, is up high.

The Confederate Army is down below.

It's a landscape in blue and gray.

What's odd—in a good way, so far as we're concerned—is that no one's fighting.

Not yet.

It's just past dawn. Everyone's getting ready, and keeping a wary eye on each other.

But not shooting.

Not yet.

We know a huge battle is going to take place sometime this day. When, exactly, I'm not sure.

The soldiers ahead of us turn in formation to the left. There's a lot of shouting and barking out of orders. Older, fatter guys, wearing sergeant's stripes, are doing the yelling. Younger, thinner guys do the marching.

Watching over all this is one of the generals we saw the night before, General Hancock, the guy with the bushy goatee. He's on a big black horse. He's personally deploying these troops, and though he didn't seem to like much of what Old Snapping Turtle had to say, he is directing these fresh troops to the middle of the line.

Which means right where we're standing is where General Pickett is going to be charging *to*.

"Um, I really think we should keep going," I say. "I mean, I really, really, really think we should keep going."

"These guys are moving to the left," says Brandon.

"That's because they're soldiers, Brandon. This is the last place in the world we want to be. This is going to be ..." I hesitate. I'm not trying to freak them out or anything.

"Is going to be what, Mel?" says Brandon.

"It's going to get pretty bad," I say. "We probably shouldn't even be *allowed* to be anywhere close. Know what I mean?"

"Allowed?" says Bev. "Since when have we been worried about that? Did we get official permission to be *allowed* in the White House? Or *allowed* to cross the Delaware with General Washington? I don't think so, Mel."

"Yeah, but this is different. I think there are some things we don't need to see. Let's keep moving, guys. The town can't be too far away."

We keep walking up the Taneytown Road. There are an amazing number of soldiers everywhere, on both sides of the road, all of them dressed in Union blue.

At the bottom of Cemetery Hill, the town of Gettysburg begins and we see a dozen or so buildings, but no one is dumb enough to be hanging around. The streets are dead quiet. It's like walking into a ghost town.

Creepy.

"Why am I getting the feeling that we're being watched?" Bev says.

"But it doesn't seem like anyone's around," says Brandon.

"That's exactly my point, Mr. State-the-Obvious. It doesn't *seem* like anyone's around. But they are. I can feel them watching me. Right at this very moment."

"That's crazy," I say, but I feel it too.

Eyes.

All over us. Watching our every footstep.

"Where we going again?" Brandon says.

"The Gettysburg Hotel," I say.

"Which is where, exactly?"

"Up ahead," I say with confidence, though the truth is I don't have a clue where the Gettysburg Hotel is.

The thing is, I just want to keep supplying Bev and Brandon simple, straightforward answers, so that they keep walking with me. It doesn't matter if I'm right or wrong. What matters is that they *think* I know what I'm doing.

Right?

It's all about confidence, you see. Because once you can fake confidence, you can fake anything.

So for a second I feel kind of good about myself. We're here, aren't we? We've made it this far, to the town of Gettysburg, haven't we? So we've done good, right?

The answers, in case you're keeping track, are as follows: *yes, yes,* and *wrong.*

The *wrong* comes in when a voice yells out.

"Hold it," the voice says. "Hold it right there, you three. Don't move a muscle. Or we'll shoot."

# THIRTY-FOUR

W E HOLD IT.

"Now put your hands on your heads," comes the voice. It's a deep voice. So deep, I start to have my suspicions, but the voice cuts in. "You try something, you die. Now state your business."

"Whose side you on?" I say. "The Blue or the Gray?"

"Whose side *you* on?" comes the voice.

"I asked you first," I say.

"But we're holding the weapons. And we should have asked you first. Just didn't think of it." The voice isn't quite as deep as it was. It's quite a few notches higher, as a matter of fact.

"All right, I'll tell you whose side we're on, and you tell us how old you are," I say. "Deal?"

A consultation takes place. I can hear voices, and none of them are deep, manly, or soldierly.

While they consult, I take a peek. Just as I suspected. Kids.

Younger than us, even.

Two of them. One boy, one girl. And they're holding broomsticks, not weapons.

"We can relax," I tell Bev and Brandon. "It's just a couple of little kids."

"Boo!" says Brandon, and fakes a jump at them. They tremble a smidgen, maybe, but don't retreat.

The girl is trying hard to come off tough. She's wearing a hat, and she's smeared dirt on her face, but she can't be older than eight or nine, or much taller than four feet.

"We got real weapons," says the boy. He's maybe a year or two older than the girl, and his face and hands are also covered with dirt. He might be closer to five feet. "We got real weapons. We're just saving 'em. Now state your business."

"First of all, are you with the Blue or the Gray?" I ask.

"Why, that's a stupid question. We live here, so we're with the Union. What about you three?"

"The Union," we say in unison.

"So state your business already. We ain't got all day."

Well, what's the harm? "We're trying to find the Gettysburg Hotel," I say. "Know where it is?"

"I might," he says. "But what's it to you?"

"You want to know our business, right? Our business is waiting for us. At the Gettysburg Hotel."

"What kind of business?"

"I can't tell you that. Not unless you decide to help us."

The boy steps forth and walks around us, as if examining the merchandise.

"Let me ask you something," I say. "You got a name?"

"Course I do," he says.

"What is it?"

He stops to consider whether or not this is something he wishes to impart. "Benjamin," he finally says.

"Really? Like in Benjamin Franklin?"

"No, like in Benjamin Stafford. My pap."

"Oh. Too bad. Benjamin Franklin was kind of like a friend of mine."

"What you say?"

"Nothing. Never mind. What's your friend's name?"

"She's not my friend; she's my sister. Now state your business at the Gettysburg Hotel."

"We need to meet someone," I say. "But things might not go as well as planned. It would be good if we could find two or three people to act as lookouts. Reliable people."

The tough-looking little girl speaks up. "We're reliable, mister. You aimin' to pay?"

"Maybe. If we could find the right people, we'd give them one whole gold coin. That's real money, not paper money."

"I ain't gonna believe you got a gold coin unless I see it with my own two eyes," Benjamin says.

I think we could probably find the hotel on our own, but I have a feeling these guys are going to come in handy. I take a coin out of my pocket, hold it up. It glints in the morning sunlight.

The girl tries to snatch it from my fingers, but Brandon catches her arm.

"Not so fast, little girl," he says.

"My name's Katie!" she says. "And I'm not so little!"

"Maybe not," Bev says. "But unless you settle down, you'll never get the coin. You'll have to earn it first, right, Mel?"

"Right, Bev," I say. "Now, which way to the Gettysburg Hotel? You'll get the gold once you take us there. Not before."

"All right," Benjamin says. "But you better keep your end of the deal, or else. Follow us." He grabs his sister's hand and begins walking. "You have to stick to the sides of buildings," he says. "On account of the Reb snipers. They took the town two days ago. And they ain't letting anyone come in or go out. Surprised they didn't shoot you three already."

As we walk up the street, Benjamin tells us that their parents owned a house and business all in one: a saddle store. The place was confiscated by Confederate officers, but their parents and two older brothers, ages twelve and fourteen, took exception. The Confederates dragged the four of them away.

"The Rebs have the whole town," Katie says. "And they ain't nice people. They tried to give my pa something they called script, but he wouldn't take it, not for anything. Pa said, 'You pay in gold or silver, or you be on your way.' They was wanting stuff for their horses, saddles and stirrups and things they said was all broken up, and Pa said, 'You want it, you pay for it.'"

"They took what they wanted anyway," says Benjamin. "And never paid, not even with that worthless script of theirs. We're aimin' to find out where they brought our pa and ma and our brothers. One thing I'm sure of, they're not at no Gettysburg Hotel."

"They'll show up," says Brandon. "This thing will be over in a day or two. Then these Confederates will be out of here. They won't be coming back either. Not ever."

"What makes you say that, mister? Everyone in town thinks it's just a matter of time before the Rebs overrun the Union Army and smash up everything."

"Yeah, well, everyone doesn't know a thing," Brandon says. "We do."

We've marched up the street, and before us is a traffic circle, ringed by the finest buildings we've seen so far. This must be the center of town. Benjamin points: "There it is," he says. "The Gettysburg Hotel."

It's a good-looking white stone building, seven or eight stories high, with a four-columned portico in front.

It doesn't look closed, and it doesn't look open.

That's concern number one.

Concern number two is I'm getting the same funny feeling Bev was getting. That someone's watching us.

"I don't think we should go in the front," I say. "We need to *reconnoiter.*" I love saying that word—I started using it last century, I believe. I ask Benjamin, "Can we get behind the hotel? Is there a back entrance?"

Benjamin gives me a curt yes with his head, and points ahead. If I understand him correctly, we need to keep going, hit the traffic circle, bear to our left, and go around the back.

Two minutes later, we're on a street behind the hotel.

"This is Race Horse Alley," Benjamin whispers. There's no one around, so there's no reason to whisper, but I get it.

We slowly walk down Race Horse Alley. After ten yards Benjamin holds up his hand. "Here you are," he says. "The back door to the Gettysburg Hotel. Now pay up."

I reach into my pocket, take out a coin, put it in his hand. I have three coins left, I remind myself.

"Wait here," I tell Benjamin and Katie. "For fifteen minutes. If you do, I'll give you another coin."

They are both looking over the coin to make certain it's real. They seem satisfied. "Wait for what?" Benjamin asks.

"For us," I say. "We might still need you."

The back door doesn't look so scary. Brandon walks up to it, grabs the handle, and pulls.

It flings wide open.

"I know a trap when I see one," says Bev. "And this is a trap."

"Does anybody have any alternatives?" I ask.

I check each face, one after the other. I don't think there's a bright idea among us.

"Well, okay then," I say. "Shall we?"

And I'm the first one through.

# THIRTY-FIVE

I T'S DARK.

No lights, no lanterns, no candles. And we're not using the flashlight on our phones, because it will drain our batteries too much.

The door opens onto a small brick-lined hallway. Dirt floor. This must be the service entrance. I can tell, because it smells like rotten food is nearby.

We have the light from outside for maybe ten feet at best. After that we're on our own.

"Know where we're going, Mel?" says Bev, who is right behind me.

"Yep," I say, again using the theory that the more I don't know, the less I should say about it. "Straight ahead."

As we lose the light and enter the darkness, Bev puts

her hand on my shoulder. I can't say for sure, but I think—and I hope—that Brandon puts his hand on Bev's shoulder the same way. We're all in. Tied together.

I kind of like it. Bev's hand gives me a little extra courage, somehow.

I have a feeling I'm going to need it.

Ten more steps and it's pitch black. *This hallway should be lit up,* I'm thinking. *There ought to be gas lanterns, candles, something.* It's almost as if someone knew we'd be coming through and made sure we'd be doing so in total darkness.

"Mel!" hisses Brandon, from behind Bev. "What's up?"

"Shhhh," I say back.

"Okay, but where are we going?"

I see a very steep and narrow staircase to our right. "Ready, everyone?" I say.

"For what?" says Brandon.

"For anything," I say, and take the first step on the first stair.

It creaks like crazy, naturally. It's so loud it would wake the dead.

The second step is worse.

"Um, Mel?" says Bev. "Any idea what we're going to do? When we get up top?"

"None," I say. "But we really ought to think of something. Now would be good."

We take four, five, six more steps, each one creakier and noisier than the last. We're about halfway home now. Or halfway to doom, depending on what happens.

We keep going, because there's no turning back at this point. Finally we come to the top.

The plan?

The one we were supposed to have come up with somewhere along the way?

It's nowhere in sight. We don't have a plan, we don't know what we're getting into, and we don't know how to get out.

"Um, Mel?" says Bev. "Now what?"

"Now we reconnoiter," says Brandon. "Right, Mel?"

"Right," I say.

We are now on the first floor of the Gettysburg Hotel. We see the lobby, the front door, the porch, a library, the dining room, and the kitchen.

Everything's been sort of trashed. Confederates must have run through the place, but no one picked up after them.

"We know Kurtis was here," I say. "That's how he would have gotten hotel stationery, right?"

"Fine," Brandon says. "Kurtis was here. So?"

"So, maybe he was a guest. He has to sleep and eat. I bet he got himself a room."

"I see where you're going with this," Bev says, hurrying across the lobby. "If he got himself a room, he must have checked in." She walks around the hotel check-in counter, finds the guest register. It doesn't take her long to spot it.

"A Mr. Albert Einstein checked in two days ago," she says. "Room 313."

Albert Einstein? Only someone born *way* after the Civil War would think to use that name.

"Clever," I say. "Let's go."

Ten seconds later, we tiptoe up the central staircase.

Twenty seconds later, we're on the third floor. Room 313 is the last room. We press our ears to the door.

No sounds, no movement within, no nothing.

I very gingerly grab hold of the doorknob, twist ever so slightly—but it's locked. And of course in 1863 they don't have magnetic cards that you can swipe to unlock the door. So either we need a key or we're going to have to break the door down.

"Ideas, anyone?" I ask.

"We should have brought the key," Brandon says.

"Great idea, Brandon," Bev says. "We should have brought breakfast too. Am I the only one that's hungry?"

"Bev," says Brandon. "Once in a while you're not half as smart as you think you are. I'm talking about the keys downstairs in the lobby. Didn't you notice that humongous key ring? It's on a hook behind the front desk. Probably has every key to every room in the joint."

Bev tries to give Brandon a sort of an apology, but since it's not something she's good at, Brandon waves her off. "Never mind," he says. "Wait here. I'll be back in a minute."

This being Brandon, it takes him not one minute, but four or five. Finally he shows up, a big smile on his face, jangling the set of keys in his left hand. "Let's hope one of 'em works," he says. "There must be fifty."

It takes a while, but the twenty-sixth key we try does the trick. The door to 313 swings open.

Inside we immediately see that Kurtis has been here, all right. And probably has every intention of coming back. A laptop, a tablet, a small portable printer, and some kind of mega-battery electrical device are on a desk next to the bed.

"Whoa," says Brandon.

Also on the desk are bound folders, as if Kurtis was preparing a presentation. The title says it all: "Union Positions, Day Three."

Then, behind the bed, we hear movement.

Something alive. And, by the sounds of it, something very, very large. Before we can process what the danger might be, the danger pops up.

It's Aubrey Micawber. He's holding a very large pistol in his left hand.

"He told me you'd come," he says. "I didn't believe him, but he insisted that you are remarkably resourceful children. Unfortunately for your sakes, we at the Pinkerton Agency have a motto: We always get our man. In this case, we always get our rather annoying children as well."

# THIRTY-SIX

He might be holding a pistol, which normally would give a guy an advantage, but Aubrey Micawber isn't doing so hot. He's still hidden behind the bed, but he hasn't risen—we can only see the top half of him. He's also dirty, sweaty, his clothes are torn, and he's wincing as if he's in great pain. His grip on the pistol is nothing to write home about either. His hand shakes so bad that it would be a minor miracle if he actually shot at something and hit it.

"Mr. Micawber," Bev says. "We should have figured."

"Perhaps. But you did not." He winces again, as if a vast pain has swept over him. His eyes shut as the wave passes over.

"You all right over there, Mr. Micawber?" I ask.

"Don't," he gasps, "worry yourselves over me. And

before we continue, I must ask: why did you sneak into General Meade's headquarters last night? I distinctly saw you do so. Do not deny it."

"To get something," I say. "That your client left behind. Do you have any idea what it was?"

"I quite assure you, young man, that my client could not possibly have left anything behind, as you say, at General Meade's headquarters. Why ever would he do so? It is a completely preposterous notion." His face scrunches up again, and he almost drops the pistol.

"What is wrong with you, Mr. Micawber?"

"There is nothing wrong with me!" he says. "But I insist you tell me the truth about last night, straightaway! These lies are too much to bear."

"He intended to blow the place up, believe it or not," I say. "Luckily it didn't work. And now he's off to do some other dirty work. Where is he, by the way?"

"I do not believe that information is of any importance to you. Mr. Kurtis has warned me that you might arrive here, and he has given me precise instructions as to what I should do in this eventuality. Now each of you will lie on the floor. On your stomachs. Please do so now, before there is any further trouble."

"Did you look at the stuff on the desk?" Bev asks. "Have you any idea what any of this is?" She holds up the tablet.

"You will put that down, young miss. That is private property and of no concern to you."

"How about this?" Brandon says, picking up the

laptop. He opens it up and turns it on. We wait a second, and then the screen turns from white to bright red. And then the letters T.G.W., Inc. in black.

"This will be your last warning," Aubrey says, waggling his pistol back and forth. "You are not to touch private property."

"But you at least have to look at this one," I say, grabbing the presentation folder. "It looks like our friend Kurtis—or *Mr.* Kurtis, as you call him—has made a couple of extra copies. 'Union Positions, Day Three.' Do you have any idea what this is about? If you don't, I might be able to fill you in. Your client is a traitor to the Union cause, Mr. Micawber. If you didn't know before, now you do. Are you sure that's okay with the Pinkerton Agency?"

He hesitates. I think everything is starting to disorient him. He looks at the assembled computer gear as if he's noticing it for the first time, and probably none of it makes sense.

I open up the presentation booklet, start reading from page 1. "'My Dear General Lee: I give you this assessment of the Union position as of seven a.m. this morning. General Meade has concluded that your next attack will be at his center, as you have failed to break through on either his northern or his southern flank. Consequently he has sent reinforcements to hold the center line, and through the night the Army's II Corp, led by the very able and determined General Winfield Scott Hancock, has been able to put in place an impregnable fortress. Keep in mind, sir, that they hold the high ground here as well; any type of frontal assault is doomed to defeat.'"

"Give me that," Aubrey says. "Bring it to me. And do not try anything. I swear I will shoot if necessary." I bring the folder over, and I see why he is crouching behind the bed: something bad has happened to his right leg.

He sees that I've noticed. "I have broken my ankle," he says. "And possibly my shoulder and my elbow, on the right side. Most unfortunate. Mobility is a wonderful thing, I've come to realize. I surely will appreciate it once I regain it. Now start turning the pages, and hold it so I can read. I am down to one usable hand, and that, sadly, I must reserve for this." He waggles the pistol. "Now turn the page."

He reads for a minute, then says, "I find this difficult to comprehend, indeed I do. Very difficult."

"So how'd you break your ankle?" Brandon says.

"I fell, if you must know," Aubrey says. "This isn't going well, I must say. When I file my report with the Pinkerton Agency . . . I'm not quite sure what I shall say."

"I don't get it," Bev says. "If you broke your ankle, what are you doing here? Shouldn't you see a doctor?"

"This is war, young lady. I will not allow myself to be treated by any war doctors. They know one method and one method only: the saw. That is most assuredly not for me."

"So . . . your plan is to lie behind a bed?"

"We were quite certain that someone would appear, sooner or later. Meanwhile I was . . . posted. To guard the room. Nothing must be taken. I am to guard each item with my life. Or those were his instructions, at any rate. Very firm he was indeed."

"You mean Kurtis?"

"Yes."

"You didn't know any better," I say. "You were given instructions, you've followed them to the letter. You did your job, but how were you to know that the guy who hired your company is an out-and-out traitor?"

"You didn't know," Brandon says.

"You couldn't," says Bev. "You've been duped. But now you have a chance to do the right thing."

"You can start by telling us exactly where Kurtis is. Or where he's going. And we'll make sure you get some help, Mr. Micawber. But we need to know pretty quick—the fate of the Union is in the balance." I nod toward the presentation in my hands. "You have all the evidence you need, sir. Now it's time to make a choice."

He sighs, another wave of pain crosses his face, and then he shakes his head. "It is he who caused my fall," he finally says. "Last night. He told me we must run, as fast as ever we could. No doubt—if what you say is true—he expected General Meade's headquarters to be blown to bits. But it was dark, and we were lost, and when we couldn't exactly see what was before us he instructed me to go first. I ran straight into a gully—a good ten-foot drop or so. I first broke my ankle, then landed on my shoulder and elbow. Having learned from my mistake, Mr. Kurtis cautiously scrambled down the side. We somehow managed to get me here, and I have been in this room ever since."

"But where did Kurtis go?"

"He wouldn't tell me. He gave me this pistol and my instructions to guard the room with my life. But I do believe I know where he has gone."

We wait for him to tell us.

"And that would be . . . ," I say.

"I do not support the Confederacy," he says. "I never have."

"Understood," I say.

"I did what I did under false pretenses," he says. "I was tricked."

"We get it," Bev says. "Now are you going to tell us where Kurtis went or what?"

"He must be on his way," Aubrey says, "to the headquarters of General Robert E. Lee."

We take this in.

General Robert E. Lee. The general in charge of the Confederate Army.

"So now comes the hard part," I say. "The hardest part of all."

"Which is what?" says Brandon.

"Now we are going to have to get to Kurtis before Kurtis gets to General Lee. Everything—and I mean *everything*—depends on it. And if we don't get there before he does, two bad things happen: one, the South wins. Two, we're stuck here forever."

"He left fifteen minutes ago," says Aubrey. "I suggest you hurry."

# THIRTY-SEVEN

So the future of the Union comes down to a fifteen-minute head start?

Fifteen short, lousy minutes?

That doesn't seem right somehow.

I could waste fifteen minutes easy. I wouldn't even break a sweat.

But now we have the opposite problem on our hands. Kurtis left fifteen minutes ago, and I have no idea how we're going to catch up.

We leave Aubrey Micawber to his own problems. Brandon yells, "Thanks!" and we run down the corridor, down the stairs, across the lobby, down the basement stairs, and we're out of the Gettysburg Hotel—that took us maybe forty seconds.

Luckily our little friends, Benjamin and Katie, are still waiting for us at the back entrance to the Gettysburg Hotel.

"Thanks for waiting," I say, handing over the extra gold coin I promised them. "Now can you tell us which way to General Lee's headquarters?"

"General Lee's headquarters?" says Benjamin. "I thought you said you was on the Union side!"

"We are," I say, knowing that every second spent explaining something is a second lost. "You have to trust us. You know where it is or not?"

"Everyone knows where ol' General Lee is. Pa told us he's holed up at the Widow Thompson's place, about a mile or two up the Chambersburg Pike. It's a nice brick mansion alongside the road. Why?"

"We need to get there fast," says Bev. "Can you rent us a horse or two? That might help."

"Nope. There ain't no horses nowhere, and we'd know, right, Katie? Pa being in the business and all. Them Rebs took every one we had, some that was sick even. Not a single live horse in all Gettysburg."

"Never mind!" I say. "Which way to the Chambersburg Pike?"

"Straight ahead." He points up Race Horse Alley. "You'll meet up with it. But you best keep an eye out— them Rebs posted snipers up in the top floors!"

"Take these," I say, giving him the last of my gold coins. "Get a doctor. There's a man in Room 313 who needs help!"

And then we're off and running. After a half mile or so—it's hard to tell how far—we come to another road, which we hope is the Chambersburg Pike.

No Reb sniper shot comes our way, or at least not that I notice. We run zigzag fashion just in case, which isn't as fun as you might think, especially after the first couple of minutes.

No street names, no traffic lights, no markers. Just a wide dirt road stretching out before us, with debris and junk scattered everywhere, which is what happens when an army comes through.

But the biggest problem is that there's no sign of Kurtis. He might even have more than fifteen minutes on us by now.

We're running as fast as we can. My side is aching and my feet are sore. I can't remember the last time I ran so hard for so long.

Yes, I can.

Never.

Bev and Brandon are just as bad.

We need to take a break, but no one can speak. We huff and puff and grimace and moan, which probably wastes a good two minutes right there.

"Are you sure we're going the right way?" Bev asks, which doesn't help.

"I think so," I say. "He said to go straight ahead. I didn't see any other roads around. And nobody else to ask directions."

"So you're hoping," says Bev.

"Got a better idea, Bev?" I say.

"No need to get all touchy, Mel. I'm just asking. Guys are so *strange* when it comes to directions."

"Chill, you two," says Brandon. "Fighting among ourselves won't help. The kid said it was a mile or two, right? We've gone at least that far."

"Where *are* we?" Bev says, looking around. On either side of this wide dirt road we see farmland, rolling hills, and not much else. "This is like the middle of *nowhere*. I think we're lost, guys. I seriously doubt that General Lee or anyone else is going to have his headquarters around here."

"Benjamin said it was up here," I say. "He'd have no reason to lie, would he?"

"He's just a *kid*, Mel," Bev says, maybe forgetting that we're all of twelve. Still, she has a point. Can we take the word of a nine-year-old?

The only thing I know is we're the only ones around who can do the job.

So we *can't* fail, is my point. Because if we do, what will happen to President Lincoln? He won't go down in history as one of our greatest presidents. He'll go down as our Biggest Loser. And the blame will be totally on us.

"It's got to be up ahead," I say. "I can't run anymore, but you know what, guys? I'm going to run anyway."

So I do. At first my bones are creaking and my muscles are protesting, but after a hundred yards or so I start to feel better. In the next hundred yards I start to actually feel almost good. I don't have enough energy to turn around, but I'm pretty sure Bev and Brandon found something extra as well. Because I hear huffing and puffing and feet scraping along the road right behind me.

The road starts to rise a little, which makes the running harder, but at this point no obstacles are going to make any difference. We're going to keep running until we can't.

At the top of the rise, the road levels off, and then we maybe see something. Way, way far ahead.

It's not a brick mansion along the side of the road.

Nor is it a solitary guy from the twenty-first century searching for General Robert E. Lee.

Nope.

What we see is a cloud of dust, heading straight at us. The kind of dust you might expect to see from a cavalry charge.

# THIRTY-EIGHT

"**I**'M GETTING A BAD feeling about this," Brandon says as the dust cloud approaches.

"So am I," says Bev.

"Me too," I say. "Should we run?"

"Run where?" says Bev. "It's this road, and farmland. We've nowhere to go."

They're fifty yards away now, and we can make them out: five men, five horses. And not just any men, either.

Confederates. Dressed in gray uniforms. Swords, boots, hats. It takes them less than a minute to circle us. And among them is our old friend from the train stoppage, Captain Rufus T. Buford.

"Whoa, whoa, whoa," says Captain Buford, holding up a white-gloved hand. "Whoa. Hmm, what have we here?

Mr. Brandon, I do believe, and his young friends. Now, y'all must know there's no traveling permitted along this particular portion of the Chambersburg Pike. None at all. This road must be clear at all times and must stay clear at all times. You ain't the first we found out here—we got a farmhouse full of folk who thought it a good idea to wander around. Which is where we're going to have to bring you folk. Those are my orders, Mr. Brandon. Sorry. You shouldn't have come down this road in the first place. Round 'em up, boys."

"But you can't do that, Captain Buford!" says Brandon. "We've . . . we've got important business! Tell him, Mel!"

"We do!" I say. "Real important!"

"Down this here road?" Captain Buford asks. "What kind of important business could you—you young ones—possibly have?"

"Our grandparents live a mile away!" I say. It's the best I can come up with on short notice. "We have to help them. Get away, that is. They're too old to leave by themselves."

"I see," Captain Buford says. "And you are all related?"

"Yes," I say.

"No," says Bev.

"What?" says Brandon.

"We're cousins," I say. "My parents didn't think I should go alone. So they asked my cousins to come."

"Interesting," says Captain Buford. "And your parents sent you three children instead of themselves because . . ."

"They're sick," I say. "Both my ma and my pa. Sick, sick, sick. And when we got word that there was going to be this gigantic battle at Gettysburg, right where my grandparents live . . . well, someone has to help, right?"

"Perhaps," Captain Buford. "If your story is true, perhaps. We are hearing some mighty strange stories. Don't have time to figure which is true and which is not. We're going to do with you three what we did with the rest. I say again, round 'em up, boys. Let's go!"

Captain Buford's men don't wait. One grabs me, one grabs Bev, and one grabs Brandon, and we're hauled up onto their horses. Then they wheel their horses around, and we gallop up the Chambersburg Pike, dust flying.

My first thought is, *Riding beats running, and since we're going in the direction we wanted to go, maybe this isn't all bad.*

My second thought is, *Depending what they do with us.*

It doesn't take long to find out. We see, perhaps a hundred yards away, a handsome brick mansion along the side of the road, just as our small friend Benjamin described. General Lee's headquarters. Any number of Confederate officers and men are riding up, riding away, milling around. But instead of riding up to the headquarters, we cut across farmland until we come to an old red barn. Surrounding it are maybe ten Confederate soldiers.

"End of the line," Captain Rufus T. Buford shouts. "Let 'em off, boys, let 'em off." Brandon and Bev slide down their horses like pros. I kind of slide-fall—getting off a horse isn't as easy as it looks. We're immediately grabbed by Confederate soldiers. "Keep an eye on these children!" says Captain Buford. He points at me. "Especially this one here. He's got himself a notion that he has to help his grandparents. You make sure that never happens, you understand?"

The solider nods his head and pulls me by the arm toward the barn door. I can see fifteen, twenty people inside, peering out; armed Confederate guards make sure no one steps outside.

"You can't . . . you can't just leave us here!" Brandon shouts. "It's not fair!"

"Oh my, you are right about that, young Mr. Brandon," Captain Buford says. "Nothing in war is fair. But I got a feeling things up here in Gettysburg will be wrapped up pretty good before this day is done. Enjoy your stay, you hear?"

Then Captain Buford turns on his horse and gallops off. The soldiers push us inside the barn and close the door.

We're the only kids. The people inside must be town-folk or local farmers who apparently either got unlucky or didn't have enough sense to stay clear of enemy soldiers.

"They're fixing on burning down the whole town when they leave," says a man. He's dressed in overalls, and has very large and ugly feet. No boots. I look at the other folks—same deal. No boots, no shoes. Taken, I guess, by shoe-deprived Confederates.

"I overheard 'em," the man continues. "Every building, they'll burn to a crisp. On account of we ain't been friendly folk. You ever hear such a thing?"

"No," I say, as the man seems to be talking to me. Other people have approached Brandon and Bev, and all of them are looking at our clothes—and especially our sneakers.

"Them's strange things on yer feet," he says. "Mind if I try 'em on?"

Oh, but I do. I inch away, and I see Brandon and Bev inching away from their questioners—if there were anywhere to run, we'd run.

But there isn't. They inch forward, we inch back, and just when we're about out of room, we hear, in this exact order, a scream, a crash, and a thud.

It's coming from the back of the barn. Then sounds of a scuffle.

Then nothing.

"I think we should check this out," I say to the man in front of me. I don't wait for an answer. I slip under his arm and head to the back of the barn, along with Bev and Brandon, who've employed the same maneuver. It gets darker the farther along we go. We hear someone moaning, and not in a good way.

Then, a light shines.

A very peculiar kind of light, considering where and when we are.

Not candle. Not gas.

Light from an app on an iPhone.

"Hello, boys and girls," says Kurtis, adjusting the Confederate officer uniform. Looks like he just stripped it from the man lying on the ground in front of him, who has a huge gash on his forehead. Kurtis shines the light from the phone on his own face. He is holding, in his other hand, a long, gleaming sword. "I've been expecting you."

# THIRTY-NINE

"**I** AM IN NEED OF assistance," Kurtis says, in a low, intimidating voice. But no matter how hard he tries, he's still a shortish, plumpish twenty-something-year-old guy. I get that he's super smart, and he co-invented a time-travel app, and among other things he aims to make a billion, or maybe ten billion, bucks. If I saw him along the street or in a mall, I don't think I'd take notice. He does have the sword, though, which at the moment kind of makes all the difference. "Listen carefully. I was rounded up like everyone else—they're not letting anyone through on the Chambersburg Pike. But I anticipated this problem, as you can see," he says, adjusting his new Confederate uniform. "Now I require you to create a diversion. Kicking, screaming at the top of your lungs, whatever you like—just make it loud enough for the guards to be compelled to investigate. When they do, I shall be on my way. As you must have surmised by now, I have important business with General Lee."

"Yeah, we've seen it," I say. "Your report on the Union's positions for Day Three. Bring it with you, Kurtis?"

"I most certainly did," he says, tapping his chest. "Right here. And how, may I ask, have you seen it?"

"You left a copy in your room. At the Gettysburg Hotel."

"I did indeed. I also left a man there to prevent your access. Evidently he failed."

"Mr. Aubrey Micawber did not fail, Kurtis. We explained what you're doing. Now he has no intention of letting you go through with your plan. And neither do we."

"General Lee will want my report, I guarantee it. He may question its authenticity—but in the end he will want to see what I have. He will find he *must* have my information, whatever the cost. Now, you may begin your diversion. I give you two minutes."

"Why would we ever help you in any way?" Bev asks. "You must be insane. You *are* insane. No doubt about it."

"We shall see who is and who isn't. Because if you do not do what I tell you, you will remain here in 1863 forever. Never to see your parents or your friends or your school or anything else ever again. Surely you do not want that. But I am a most forgiving sort. As soon as General

Lee and I conclude our agreement, I will return access to the iTime app. For each one of you."

"And what if we say no?" says Brandon.

He swipes the air in front of us with his sword. It comes a quarter inch from my nose.

"There is more than one way to get the guards' attention," he says. "Fake screams—or real ones. Now I tell you for the final time: create a diversion. I suggest we begin with the girl. Surely she knows how to scream with fright, doesn't she? Just pretend you see a mouse. I'm sure that will do the trick."

Okay, that's two mistakes in one. Bev just isn't the screamy type. And two, as far as mice goes, she *likes* them. They're great for . . . experiments and stuff—in the lab.

"You . . . ," says Bev. Her eyes narrow; her lips tighten. I know she's trying real hard to come up with exactly the right word here. "You . . ."

He lunges at us before she can think of it, which I don't think is very sporting of him, or gentlemanly. Then he slashes with that sword. I snap my head back, and this time he comes within an eighth of an inch from my nose—so close it kind of tickles. But while I'm going backward and Kurtis is going forward, Brandon and Bev attack. Brandon tackles him from the front, and Bev from the side.

I think maybe Bev bites him one, right in his thigh.

They all go down.

I jump in on top. I'm really trying to get his report,

which he's keeping close to his chest. I claw for it with both hands, and Kurtis stiff-arms me with one hand while keeping hold of his sword with the other. Then all four of us go rolling around the barn, knocking over every farm implement and barrel in our way.

Which gets the attention of the local lost and wandering residents who've been thrown into this barn with us. They shuffle over at first. It takes them a second to compute what's going on, but when it registers, they like what they see and start yelling, "Fight, fight, fight!"

Since it's dark at our end of the barn, and also because Brandon and Bev and me are in the mix, it takes them a second to notice that Kurtis is dressed as a Confederate officer.

"It's a Reb!" shouts one. "Get 'im!" shouts another. Before long, twenty folks are jumping on Kurtis, giving him what for.

"Get off me, you dirty creeps!" Kurtis manages to sputter. "Get off me or I swear . . ."

Brandon, who has a sense of how to handle himself during these types of things, tries to wrench the sword from Kurtis's hand, but Kurtis is stronger than he looks and won't let go. All this screaming and kicking and wrenching does serve his original purpose, though—it's created a diversion. A big one. Big enough to get the attention of our Confederate guards, who throw open the doors to the barn and rush into the fray.

At first the guards must be thinking that we, the

scattered citizenry of Gettysburg, are merely fighting among ourselves. Then they see, in the middle of the pile, the uniform of a Confederate officer.

Their attitude changes. Not in a good way either.

The soldiers start yelling and swinging their rifles, which clears a path pretty quick to Kurtis, who's lying on the ground with a bloody nose and Brandon still trying to wrest his sword away. Then a loud, booming, commanding voice yells, "Stop! Stop this instant, I say! Or I will see you all hanged!"

It is Captain Rufus T. Buford.

"What in the name of old Virginny is going on in this barn?" Then he notices Kurtis, who is rising to his feet and dusting himself off.

"You, sir! What is your name, and who is your commanding officer?"

"Lieutenant William C. McConnell, sir!" Kurtis says, snapping off a smart salute. I immediately get the feeling that Kurtis was ready for the question and ready with his answer. "I am on General Lee's staff, sir, and I have retrieved most important information from a spy I have been carefully cultivating. These people here"—Kurtis points to us all, as if we're the lowest form of riffraff imaginable—"are trying to interfere with my work. Now I beseech you, sir, escort me immediately to General Lee! My news is urgent! The fate of the Confederacy is at stake!"

# FORTY

I GUESS I CAN'T BLAME HIM.

Captain Rufus T. Buford, that is.

You see, he doesn't know that Kurtis is an impostor and a cheat and an evildoer and an all-around bad dude. Captain Buford only sees what's before him and hears what he hears.

So he instantly accepts "Lieutenant McConnell" as a fellow Confederate in need of rescuing. It's understandable.

I didn't say good. But understandable.

He gets Kurtis out of there on the double-quick.

"I shall personally escort you, Lieutenant, to General Lee!" Captain Buford cries. "Now the rest of you—back, I say, back! Or else you'll be the first Yankees we shoot this day!"

We can do nothing but watch as first Captain Buford and Kurtis leave, then the guards leave, and then the barn door is closed and locked, leaving the three of us and about twenty townies together again.

They're not going to be much help. They stare at us and we stare at them for a few seconds and then the real Confederate officer who was relieved of his uniform by Kurtis starts to come around.

"Who's he?" says a man dressed in overalls.

"Just a guy," I say. "But it's good." I motion with my fingers for them to go. "No worries."

They slowly drift off, one by one, to the front of the barn, where rays of sunlight are streaming through the slats in the wall. I think the sunbeams comfort them, because nearly all of them find one to stand in.

"We have to get out of here," I say. "Like, now. We can't let Kurtis give that report to General Lee. It could change the outcome of American history." While I'm talking, I turn on the phone, just to make sure it's working more than anything else. But as soon as I do, I hear, in quick succession, *ba-da-bing, ba-da-bing, ba-da-bing*.

Incoming.

Three new texts. From Mr. Hart again, not Kurtis.

Text one: *Mel, we have regained control of messaging. Are you there?*

Text two: *Mel, REPORT!*

Text three: *Mel, OBEY THESE INSTRUCTIONS TO THE LETTER: WE HAVE REACTIVED YOUR ITIME APP!!! IT WILL ENGAGE AUTOMATICALLY*

*AT 1 P.M.!!! THIS WILL BE YOUR ONE AND ONLY WINDOW TO RETURN TO THE PRESENT!! CANCEL YOUR MISSION!! REPEAT, CANCEL YOUR MISSION AND COME BACK!!*

"One p.m.?" says Brandon. "That's like in fifteen minutes! We get to go home!" He takes out his own phone, turns it on, swipes through. "Look!" he says. "The iTime app is up!"

We all look, and yes indeed, the iTime app appears to be fully functional once again. But it's not set to activate in fifteen minutes anymore.

We're already down to fourteen.

"We have to get out of this stupid barn," I say. "At least one of us does."

"For what?" says Bev.

"To get that report," I say. "Before Kurtis can give it to General Lee."

"But Mr. Hart said to cancel the mission," Brandon says. "Didn't he?"

"Yes, he did, Brandon. But Mr. Hart doesn't know the situation. We do."

I think of what President Lincoln said—about how a few people might be called upon to defend a few yards of ground, and what they should have in the forefront of their minds at the critical moment.

To remind me, I cue up the selfie the president took—the good one. Where he's looking noble and majestic, with a faraway vision in his eye.

That moment he talked about is right here, right now.

His selfie gives me all that I need: courage, strength, inspiration. For it's come to this—I am the president's only soldier.

I scan the barn, and I see the chance. Up high. A small, open window. Too small for an adult to squeeze through. Maybe too small for Brandon to squeeze through.

But not for me.

No stairs, no second floor, though. Only one way to get there. And not a second to lose.

I run to the wall directly underneath the window and start scrambling up. It's not as hard as you might think—every four feet or so, there's a beam I can grab on to, or a ledge, or an out-of-whack plank with an inch or two of space for my foot or my fingers.

I'm halfway up before Brandon and Bev start shouting out advice. Three-quarters of the way up before the townies notice, and I'm nearly at the window before they start pointing and dropping their jaws in astonishment.

And then I'm up to the window and halfway out. "Hold on to your phones!" I yell down to Brandon and Bev. "And wait for one o'clock!"

# FORTY-ONE

I HADN'T FIGURED THAT climbing up would be the *easy* part.

Because now I have to get down.

In a hurry.

The view is good from the top of the barn, though—precarious, scary, dangerous, for sure—but you can see all around.

I see in front of me a fine brick mansion alongside the Chambersburg Pike. Emerging now from the front of the mansion are a bunch of Confederate generals—I can tell by the stripes on their shoulders. And in the middle of the generals is a white-haired old gentleman who must be General Robert E. Lee, in charge of the entire Confederate Army.

Approaching them are Captain Buford and Kurtis, who's whipped out that report of his and is waving it high in the air.

"General Lee!" Kurtis calls. "General Lee! I have something of the utmost importance to show you!"

General Lee happens to be looking, at this very moment, at his pocket watch.

I look at my phone: 12:57.

"General Lee!" cries Kurtis. "I have valuable information! Maps, enemy troop positions—everything! You must halt the attack immediately!"

General Lee looks up. I look down. A stack of hay, a few feet from the barn, is my one and only option.

Even though I can't judge how high or how deep the stack is, I can't waste a single second thinking about it. It's do-or-die time.

*Do.*

*Or die.*

I find my footing on the slanted roof and take a running leap.

I need to hit the target right in the middle. Two feet off this way, three feet off that way—it wouldn't be pretty. Onlookers would ask: *What is* up *with that kid? He just jumped off the roof! What an idiot!*

"Look out!" I hear someone yell.

"Watch it!" yells someone else.

On my way down I see General Lee's eyes look up and follow my flight path. I don't know who's more surprised—him or me—when I nail the landing with a perfect 10.

12:58.

I jump out of the haystack, Captain Buford points my way, Kurtis charges ahead, and General Lee holds up his hands.

"Shoot him!" yells Captain Buford. "He's a Yankee!"

"General Lee, sir, you must stop your attack!" yells Kurtis.

"What is all this commotion?" asks General Lee.

Kurtis is only twenty yards away now, so I pivot, put on the jets, and before he can get his pamphlet to General Lee, I snatch it from his outstretched hands.

"Shoot!" yells Captain Buford. "Shoot, I say, shoot!"

"You must not attack the Union center!" Kurtis screams. "It's all there in the pamphlet—all the details! You will be crushed!"

"Nonsense!" says General Lee, stepping off the porch and toward Kurtis. "Who are you, sir, to say such a thing!" Then he turns to the generals behind him and says, "Tell the men to proceed with the bombardment—exactly at one p.m., as scheduled!"

12:59.

"Fire at one!" yells one of the generals, and I hear, down the line, the order relayed like an echo: *Fire at one! Fire at one! Fire at one!*

"You fool!" Kurtis yells at General Lee. "Listen to me! Your army will be destroyed!"

I'm running far from them now, the pamphlet in my hand, and Kurtis is torn between chasing me and standing at attention for General Lee, who is fast approaching him, his face red with anger. "I have never seen fit to call another man a fool to his face!" General Lee says. "That you do so to a superior officer is an abomination!"

"Shoot!" yells Captain Buford.

"Fire!" yells General Lee. "It is time!"

And right on cue, the biggest, loudest, most thunderous bombardment on U.S. soil commences.

A thousand July Fourth firework grand finales rolled into one wouldn't come close.

The ground literally shakes, like a monumental, 7.0-on-the-Richter-scale earthquake. My ears split with the noise.

It's the enormous artillery barrage that precedes, as I recall, the infamous failed charge of General George Pickett.

On the one hand, all is well, because what's supposed to happen actually *is* happening, despite all of Kurtis's efforts to the contrary. Mission accomplished, in other words. President Lincoln, if he knew, would be very, very happy. And we'll take whatever applause, congratulations, donations, etc., come our way, but—believe me—we're not expecting much.

However, on the other hand? The last time Captain Buford said "Shoot," I suspect someone shot.

At me, to be precise.

That, then, is the last thing I see: General Lee's stern, angry face; Captain Buford, sword in hand, pointed my way; Kurtis, pleading his case; the generals behind them shouting out the order to fire; and, from the corner of my eye, a lone Rebel, rifle raised, finger on the trigger, a puffball of smoke.

The bullet halfway home . . .

# FORTY-TWO

I'M HIT—OR I'M vaporized. Hard to tell at first.

Then I think it through. If I had been hit by a bullet from a Confederate rifle, I'd be feeling tremendous pain, right? In my neck, shoulder, stomach—someplace.

But I feel no pain whatsoever. Quite the contrary. I feel—well, I don't want to go overboard or anything, but I'm getting kind of an ecstatic vibe, if you want to know the truth.

It's like supreme happiness suddenly hits me like a truck—but in a good way.

I'm ecstatic because I actually dodged a real live bullet. And ecstatic because if all my calculations are correct, and I think they are, then we just totally saved the Union.

I want to high-five someone. Shout yippee at the top of my voice.

Unfortunately, you can't high-five anyone, not even yourself, when you're doing that time-travel-in-the-space-time-continuum deal. All your bits and pieces are not exactly *there*. Every molecule you possess has been deconstructed and is awaiting reassembly. But even though I don't have hands or fingers or toes in full working order—not at the *moment* anyway—I feel the satisfaction of a mission accomplished.

We did it. I think Abe would be proud.

Any actual high-fiving is going to have to wait, though, until I'm done with the roller-coaster-in-the-darkness part.

I don't know up from down.

I feel like I'm going to lose my lunch.

Then I land on my butt with a thump.

And I'm in the basement of Taylor's General Store, at Washington Crossing. And right next to me are Brandon and Bev. On their butts like me.

"Mel!" shouts Bev.

"Dude!" shouts Brandon. "You had us worried!"

Some things just can't be stopped, like an avalanche, a runaway train, or a group hug after a do-or-die situation, even among three kids who maybe aren't exactly *friends*, but sure aren't strangers anymore, either. We jump to our feet, grab each other, laugh, holler, hop around, etc.

You get the picture.

We're happy, okay? And we *earned* it. We're alive, we're in one piece, and in case you forgot, we just saved the day again, big-time.

So it's not our fault that Professor Moncrieff, Mr.

Hart, and those three large military-type guys with the dark shades are standing around in the basement of the general store with their hands on their hips and perfectly grumpy expressions on their faces.

"Look!" I say. "I brought it with me—Kurtis's plans! He was going to give it to General Lee! But I snatched it away at the last possible second—so it's all good!"

We've stopped hopping up and down now, and we're in the process of disentangling from one another. I wave Kurtis's pamphlet back and forth, but still not a smile or a single word of praise from the Committee of Gloom.

Professor Moncrieff is the first to speak. He somehow looks even older than he did the last time we saw him, which was a hundred and fifty years ago, sort of. "Papers? You bring us papers? Why did you not bring us Kurtis? Were you not explicitly ordered to do so?"

Just then, and I swear my phone has a mind of its own and likes to chirp up at particularly awkward moments, we hear that old tri-chord melody. An incoming text from Mr. Hart. *Belay last instructions*, it says. *Grab Kurtis first, THEN return. KURTIS MUST BE BROUGHT BACK WITH YOU!!!!!*

"Belay?" says Brandon, looking over my shoulder. "What does that mean?"

"I think it means to cancel something," says Bev. "But it seems as if we got the message too late, because we're here and Kurtis is still there. But let me tell you people something: we're not going back, and that's final. If you guys want to go"—she points to the military men—"then be our guests."

"We cannot leave Kurtis free and unfettered!" says Professor Moncrieff. "There's no telling where he'll go or what he'll do next time!"

"Well, then I guess you'll have to figure something out, Professor, won't you?" Bev says. "But we've done enough. And everything's turned out just fine. You can thank us later. Right now, we're going back to school. I, for one, am taking a hot shower, and then we're going to have a Christmas dinner. Together. Mel and Brandon—does that sound like a plan, or what?"

It sure does. We link arms, nod in unison, and troop up the staircase.

"Mr. Hart?" says Brandon. "You coming? We need a ride back."

"Just a sec," Mr. Hart says. "I'll just see what the professor wants me to do."

Whatever, Mr. Hart. We walk up the stairs, fling open the basement door, and step out into the sunlight. It couldn't be a more glorious Christmas afternoon. Happy, smiling people are all around, as the festivities celebrating the Crossing of the Delaware by our old friend General George Washington are not yet over.

"Let's take the bridge," says Brandon. "Mr. Hart can pick us up on the other side." We march across the mighty Delaware River, arms linked, heads held high. I wish George and Abe could walk this bridge alongside us and see for themselves these *United* States, still standing, still strong.

"Not a bad day," I say. "First, we saved the Revolution . . ."

"And then the Union," finishes Brandon. "Just sayin'."

"But that's it," Bev says. "No more time traveling for us. Right, guys?"

"Right," we say.

Mr. Hart picks us up on the New Jersey side, and before we know it, we're home.

For good.

We hope. . . .

**LEFTOVERS**

Although I can't say I've researched every single presidential marriage—as of this writing we've had forty-three presidents, but Jefferson was a widower, Buchanan a bachelor, and Tyler, Cleveland, and Wilson married while in office—I don't think it's going too far out on a limb to suggest that Abraham and Mary Todd Lincoln's relationship is among the most curious. I am indebted to Daniel Mark Epstein's *The Lincolns: Portrait of a Marriage* for his sympathetic handling of the intimate details of their marriage.

Mary Todd Lincoln did conduct séances in the White House, and Charles J. "Lord" Colchester was indeed a real character, in all senses of the word. The death of the Lincolns' son Willie, at age eleven, had a profound effect on their marriage in general, and on Mary Lincoln in particular. Her grief was such that she not only neglected nine-year-old Tad, but was also highly receptive to charlatans who promised her spiritual communion with Willie. President Lincoln attended one or two séances himself, but while he was certainly superstitious, he was no spiritualist—he prevailed upon Joseph Henry, a prominent scientist and secretary of the Smithsonian Institution, to debunk Colchester's far-fetched claims.

If a boy such as Tad Lincoln were alive today, parental advice would most certainly cascade upon the Lincolns. Tad was impulsive, rambunctious, headstrong, and emotional; he was somewhat indulged by his father and ignored by his mother; and he was given unstructured command of his surroundings, which he naturally exploited to maximum advantage. But he was, by all accounts, basically a good-hearted boy, which may in the end be more important than anything else. For a wonderful, nonbiased portrait of the Lincoln White House, I recommend *Tad Lincoln's*

*Father* by Julia Taft Bayne, who was a childhood friend of Willie's and Tad's.

The summers in Washington City in the centuries before indoor air-conditioning were notably awful, so the Lincolns spent a good portion of July and August three miles away from the White House, in the parklike setting of the Soldiers Home, which was somewhat more open and breezy. I have taken the liberty of conveniently forgetting this fact and having the Lincolns remain in the White House so Mel, Bev, and Brandon could see it for themselves.

The Ironclad Oath did exist, as did travel passes to enter or exit Washington City. Mary Todd Lincoln was involved in a horse carriage accident, though it occurred on July 2, 1863, not July 1. She did in fact hit her head, and her son Robert later said she was never the same.

By most accounts President Lincoln was forthcoming with his wife about the progress of the war, even though she endured many accusations of being a Southern sympathizer or even a spy because many in her family sided with the Confederacy. She urged Lincoln to replace the preening General George McClellan, for example, who liked to lead his men on the parade ground but not the battlefield.

As for secret tunnels in the White House—let's say I made it up. Mostly . . .

The Battle of Gettysburg is one of the most written-about subjects in American history, and it's hard to think that anything new can be added at this stage of the game. But in 2013 Allen C. Guelzo, the Henry R. Luce III Professor of the Civil War Era at Gettysburg College, produced what I consider the definitive one-volume history of this epic battle. *Gettysburg: The Last Invasion* is a model of fact, fluency, understanding, clarity, and historical writing of the first order.

I've used "Union Army" to describe General George Meade's command, which was actually known as the Army of the Potomac. In his later years, General Meade vehemently denied that he ever considered retreating from Gettysburg to the more fortified position of Pipe Creek, Maryland. I think a fair assessment is that he certainly did think of it, and for good reasons: he believed the chances of success were better. He could not bring his generals around to his way of thinking, however, and so the battle was fought—and won—where they stood.

I visited Gettysburg for the first time on July 3, 2013—exactly 150 years after Pickett's Charge. I was with my family—we were planning on staying a few days as part holiday and part research trip—and celebrations and commemorations were taking place throughout the town and the battle site. The day was hot, bright and sunny, and the mood was festive; at first I was very pleased to be there.

Then I stood on one corner of that hallowed ground, about where General Alexander Hays's Third Division held the Union right flank. Suffice it to say that *my* mood, at least, was festive no more. I couldn't help thinking about what had occurred there on that day, on American soil, among Americans. May we never see another day like it.

*DP, Pennington, NJ*

# RECOMMENDED READING

**HISTORICAL FICTION**

Angleberger, Tom, and Michael Hemphill. *Stonewall Hinkleman and the Battle of Bull Run.* New York: Puffin, 2014.

Avi. *Iron Thunder: The Battle Between the Monitor & the Merrimac: A Civil War Novel.* New York: Hyperion, 2009.

Denslow, Sharon Phillips. *All Their Names Were Courage: A Novel of the Civil War.* New York: Greenwillow, 2003.

Durrant, Lynda. *My Last Skirt: The Story of Jennie Hodgers, Union Soldier.* New York: Clarion, 2006.

Fleischman, Paul. *Bull Run.* New York: Harper Trophy, 1995.

Harness, Cheryl. *Ghosts of the Civil War.* New York: Simon & Schuster Books for Young Readers, 2001.

Hart, Alison. *Gabriel's Horses.* Atlanta: Peachtree, 2010.

Hughes, Pat. *Seeing the Elephant: A Story of the Civil War.* New York: Farrar, Straus and Giroux, 2007.

Keehn, Sally M. *Anna Sunday.* New York: Puffin, 2004.

Murphy, Jim. *The Journal of James Edmond Pease, a Civil War Union Soldier: Virginia, 1863.* New York: Scholastic, 1998.

Philbrick, Rodman. *The Mostly True Adventures of Homer P. Figg.* New York: Scholastic, 2011.

Rinaldi, Ann. *Girl in Blue.* New York: Scholastic, 2004.

Schwabach, Karen. *The Storm Before Atlanta.* New York: Random House, 2010.

## NONFICTION

Allen, Thomas B., and Roger MacBride Allen. *Mr. Lincoln's High-Tech War: How the North Used the Telegraph, Railroads, Surveillance Balloons, Ironclads, High-Powered Weapons, and More to Win the Civil War.* Washington, D.C.: National Geographic, 2009.

Bolden, Tonya. *Emancipation Proclamation: Lincoln and the Dawn of Liberty.* New York: Abrams Books for Young Readers, 2013.

Brown, Don. *He Has Shot the President! April 14, 1865: The Day John Wilkes Booth Killed President Lincoln.* New York: Roaring Brook Press, 2014.

Freedman, Russell. *Abraham Lincoln and Frederick Douglass: The Story Behind an American Friendship.* New York: Clarion Books, 2012.

Hakim, Joy. *War, Terrible War: 1855–1865* (A History of US). New York: Oxford University Press, 2005.

Hale, Nathan. *Nathan Hale's Hazardous Tales: Big Bad Ironclad!* New York: Amulet Books, 2012.

Herbert, Janis. *The Civil War for Kids: A History with 21 Activities.* Chicago: Chicago Review Press, 1999.

Marrin, Albert. *Unconditional Surrender: U.S. Grant and the Civil War.* New York: Atheneum Books for Young Readers, 1994.

———. *Virginia's General: Robert E. Lee and the Civil War.* New York: Atheneum Books for Young Readers, 1994.

———. *A Volcano Beneath the Snow: John Brown's War Against Slavery.* New York: Alfred A. Knopf, 2014.

McPherson, James M. *Fields of Fury: The American Civil War.* New York: Atheneum Books for Young Readers, 2002.

Moss, Marissa. *Nurse, Soldier, Spy: The Story of Sarah Edmonds, a Civil War Hero.* New York: Abrams for Young Readers, 2011.

Murphy, Jim. *The Boys' War: Confederate and Union Soldiers Talk About the Civil War.* New York: Clarion Books, 1990.

———. *The Long Road to Gettysburg.* New York: Clarion Books, 1992.

Sheinkin, Steve. *Lincoln's Grave Robbers.* New York: Scholastic, 2012.

———. *Two Miserable Presidents: Everything Your Schoolbooks Didn't Tell You About the Civil War.* New York: Flash Point, 2009.

Silvey, Anita. *I'll Pass for Your Comrade: Women Soldiers in the Civil War.* New York: Clarion Books, 2008.

Stanchak, John E. *Civil War.* New York: Dorling Kindersley, 2011.

Walker, Sally M. *Secrets of a Civil War Submarine: Solving the Mysteries of the* H. L. Hunley. Minneapolis: Carolrhoda Books, 2005.

# WEBSITES OF INTEREST

**ABRAHAM LINCOLN**

Abraham Lincoln's Classroom (abrahamlincolnsclassroom.org)

Abraham Lincoln Presidency Biography
(whitehouse.gov/1600/presidents/abrahamlincoln)

Abraham Lincoln Presidential Library Foundation (alplm.org)

The Lincoln Institute (abrahamlincoln.org)

Mr. Lincoln's White House (mrlincolnswhitehouse.org)

**CIVIL WAR**

BrainPop: The Civil War—film, quizzes, activities, etc.
(brainpop.com/socialstudies/freemovies/civilwar)

Civil War@Smithsonian (civilwar.si.edu)

Civil War Trust (civilwar.org)

Civil War Washington (civilwardc.org)

National Park Service: The Civil War (nps.gov/civilwar)

National Park Service: Gettysburg National Military Park
(nps.gov/gett)

PBS's *The Civil War* by Ken Burns (pbs.org/civilwar)

The Smithsonian Associates Civil War Studies
(civilwarstudies.org)

# SITES, MUSEUMS, AND LIVING HISTORY

## ABRAHAM LINCOLN

**Abraham Lincoln's Birthplace,** also known as the first Lincoln Memorial, is located in rural Hodgenville, Kentucky. Hike Overlook Trail and walk along both Knob Creek and Sinking Spring, two of the Lincoln family's water sources. Go to nps.gov/abli to plan your visit.

The **Abraham Lincoln Presidential Library and Museum** in Springfield, Illinois, "brings to life Abraham Lincoln's story through immersive exhibits and displays of original artifacts." Learn more at illinois.gov/alplm.

Impressively situated on the National Mall in Washington, D.C., the **Lincoln Memorial** sits directly opposite the Washington Monument. Inscribed on the walls of the memorial are Lincoln's Gettysburg Address and Second Inaugural Address. You can explore the memorial's online interactive features by going to nps.gov/linc.

## CIVIL WAR

Abolitionist John Brown's raid on the armory at Harpers Ferry in 1859 served as a pivotal moment leading up to the start of the Civil War. Today, at **Harpers Ferry National Historical Park,** where the Potomac and Shenandoah rivers meet, guests may visit John Brown's Fort, take guided tours and experience living history workshops, and explore over twenty miles of hiking trails. For maps, a calendar, and additional tips, go to nps.gov/hafe.

The Civil War began at **Fort Sumter** on April 12, 1861, when the Confederacy opened fire on the military fort. Situated on an island in Charleston, South Carolina, visitors can take guided tours and view museum exhibits in the visitor centers. Before making the trip, visit nps.gov/fosu to read about accessing the fort by boat.

**Antietam National Battlefield,** in western Maryland, is the location of America's "bloodiest one-day battle," which took place in the early fall of 1862. In addition to studying the natural terrain of the battlefield, visitors can explore the restored **Dunker Church,** the **Observation Tower at Bloody Lane,** the **Pry House Field Hospital Museum,** and the **National Cemetery.** More information is available at nps.gov/anti.

Every July, the Gettysburg Anniversary Committee organizes a **reenactment of the Battle of Gettysburg** in Gettysburg, Pennsylvania, to recognize the importance of the three-day 1863 battle. Visit gettysburgreenactment.com to read the event schedule and find out how to purchase tickets. For more information about **Gettysburg National Military Park,** visit nps.gov/gett.

The Union and Confederacy battled over Chattanooga, once known as the Gateway to the Deep South, in the fall of 1863. **Chickamauga and Chattanooga National Military Park,** located in both Georgia and Tennessee, is open year-round. Visitors can hike the trails, take ranger-led tours, participate in group programs, and on summer weekends, explore the Cravens House on Lookout Mountain. Find more information at nps.gov/chch.

General Lee surrendered at the **Appomattox Court House** in Appomattox, Virginia, on April 9, 1865. Open year-round, visitors can attend special events during the April anniversary week, hike the trail, watch videos in the theater, and see artifacts on exhibit. Between Memorial Day and Labor Day, living-history programs are also offered. For more information, visit nps.gov/apco.

The **National Civil War Museum** is located in Harrisburg, Pennsylvania. Open year-round, it features self-guided and group tours, videos, life-size dioramas, and an engaging timeline of the Civil War, composed of artifacts, documents, photographs, and other material. Go to nationalcivilwarmuseum.org for more information.

For even more information on upcoming events, reenactments, and living history sites, go to civilwartraveler.com/events.

# ACKNOWLEDGMENTS

Thanks to Brian; Phoebe; Rachel; Ken; Alison; Deb Dwyer; C. F. Payne; Ginny Potter; Uncle Bruce Potter; my sons, Thomas and Charlie; and most of all my wife, Cindy